ALSO BY
MILLIE ABECASSIS

Daughters of the Blue Moon (Anuci Press)
Bright City, Shattered (Polymath Press)
A Legacy of Blood and Bone (Brick & Bloom)
The Seventh Sister (Anuci Press)

PRAISE FOR
THE COLOR OF TIME

"In this refreshingly futuristic retelling, *The Color of Time* is a revolutionary modernization of the classic fable. The whimsical charm of the original is retained through the unique narrative perspective, then elevated into **an expansive original parable of sapphic yearning, mistakes and redemption, and—most importantly—the fight for freedom.** This succinct tale is a perfect getaway for anyone looking to reconnect with a sense of wonder without sacrificing the sophistication afforded by a fast-paced political science-fantasy."

—Florence Chien, author of *The Revenant of Surolifia*

"*The Color of Time* stands as a breathtaking triumph of science fantasy. Fiercely realized characters command every chapter as they ignite a revolution to shatter the chains of tradition and tyranny. Millie Abecassis has delivered **a tour de force that pulses with political intrigue** and pioneers a daring expansion of the genre. This sweeping saga proves that the most powerful force in any galaxy is the courage to rewrite one's destiny. Don't miss this incredible new entry from a rising authorial voice."

—Jason Denzel, author of *The Mystic Trilogy*

"Filled with compelling characters, an intriguing narration, and an interstellar setting that feels both at once innovative and familiar, *The Color of Time* invites readers into a narrative that dares to explore the difficult—and oftentimes uncomfortable—choices a person might make in order to survive. The plot is tightly structured and the stakes continue to rise throughout, offering a thrilling experience that will have you up all night. Abecassis skillfully preserves a fable-like touch in this sci-fi reimagining of the Donkeyskin fairytale, making this **a wholly unique and positively delightful read!**"

— T.A. Chan, author of *The Celestial Seas*

THE COLOR OF TIME

MILLIE ABECASSIS

Published by Shiraki Press
Mill Creek, Washington, USA
First edition 2026

For information about this book, including distribution and media reviews, scan or visit:

shirakipress.com/books/the-color-of-time/

THE COLOR OF TIME
Copyright © 2026 by Millie Abecassis
All rights reserved.

ISBN: 978-1-970458-07-7 (Paperback)
ISBN: 978-1-970458-06-0 (EPUB)

Library of Congress Control Number: 2026937307

Published by Shiraki Press
P.O. Box 13394, Mill Creek, WA 98082
shirakipress.com

To Félix, who gave me the strength to
finish this story while my world fell apart.

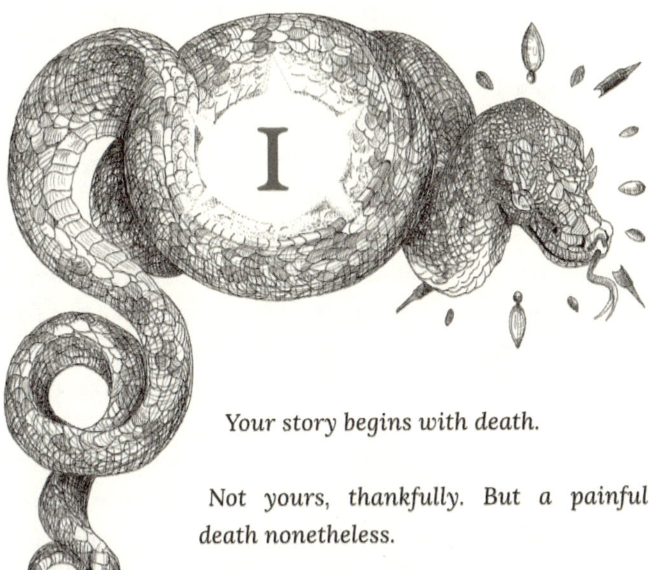

Your story begins with death.

Not yours, thankfully. But a painful death nonetheless.

Marise was dying, and there was nothing you could do about it. Everyone close to Marise, yourself most of all, knew she was a good woman. Unlike her husband, King Elias of Cicia, she could have made a decent ruler—and I'm telling you this as someone who believes all monarchs are inherently unfit to rule. If all the kings and queens and emperors and empresses walking the galaxy's planets had been as kind as Marise, perhaps I wouldn't have become the staunch republican that I am. But it doesn't matter what kind of ruler Marise could have been, because she was only the king's wife, and she was dying. What you didn't know at the time of her passing is that Marise's death was the only way for you to become Green Scales, the woman I fell in love with.

MARISE'S LOVE FOR spaceflight, the depth of which you witnessed when she brought you along, had caused irreversible damage to her body. It wasn't your fault, you knew, but you still felt guilty. Too often, you had supported her. Encouraged her. You'd ask her when she would travel next to the moon, to the nearby planets of Rebos and Eucaria, or to other systems. She'd wink at you and grab your hand before taking you to her favorite spaceship, the *Starling*, a small racing ship she always used for her personal travels.

I wish I could say you were both young and naive, but you were not. Young, yes, but you both knew the risks. Racing ships are for racing, not for lengthy spaceflights. How many solar flares happened when you were flying between your home planet of Therria and Rebos? How many cosmic rays bombarded the thin hull of the ship? *Too many*, you would say, lowering your gaze. *But it's worth it*, you'd think secretly in the back of your mind. It was worth it when Marise put her finger on her lips and gave you an impish look before activating her diastium engine—opening a wormhole through the fabric of spacetime—and taking you to planets like Onvoth, Xulia, Reon V, or Phau.

Was it really worth it? you asked yourself, holding Marise's hand as she lay in bed. *Of course not.* But you couldn't have stopped her. Even if you hadn't encouraged Marise, her passion for flying outweighed everything else. All the warnings in the world would have changed nothing. She was the one who taught you to fly, after all.

"Elias," Marise said softly, her voice barely audible in the vastness of the queen's bedchamber. "Leave us alone."

He looked at you, then at Marise, and shook his head. "You are my wife. I will not abandon you when you are at the threshold of death." Elias's voice was firm but hollow.

Marise inhaled as deeply as she could. Breathing had

become so difficult that she barely spoke anymore, precipitating her decline. Being forced into silence was, after being forced to stop flying the *Starling*, the worst thing that had happened to her.

"I only wish to receive serenity… before my passing to the Meadows. Once Cyrelle has serened me… you will come back to me for my last breath."

He nodded and left without arguing.

"Cyrelle," Marise whispered before you began the serening ritual. "Listen to me."

"I am listening," you said, squeezing her hand harder.

"I need you to make me a promise."

A promise? You didn't expect Marise to ask you this. She had never made you promise anything before. But dying people have last wishes, so you nodded and said, "Anything."

"You shall not gift serenity… to those who don't want it."

You frowned before asking, "Why would anyone refuse to be blessed by Zephis?"

"Because serenity kills your will."

"Kills your will?" you asked, uncertain. As a Serenitress yourself, you were well versed in the effects of the serening ritual, but you had never considered how it could impact someone's will.

What about yours, you wondered? You had been serened many times, by others or by yourself. Had it, somehow, influenced your own desires and your will to fulfill them? But now wasn't the time to think about yourself, so you squeezed Marise's hand, gently prompting her to respond.

"Yes," she said, before adding, slowly breathing in and out between words, "Promise me… you will never force serenity… on those who need… to keep their will strong."

For an instant, you wondered if she spoke from experience. Had you mistakenly killed Marise's will by serening her when you shouldn't have? You always serened people when they requested it, and Marise was no exception. Should you have refused her Zephis's gift for her own good? It was too late to worry about it, but at least you could become a better Serenitress. And the promise also applied to you, you guessed. The next time you wished to serene yourself, you would think twice about it.

"I promise," you said.

"Please also promise me… you won't give serenity… to those who don't deserve it."

This was an easy promise to keep, one you had already made on the day you became a Serenitress. A tear rolling down your cheek, you said again, "I promise."

FOURTHDAY 18 TERMISUN 1496 AE
HYLA, KINGDOM OF CICIA, THERRIA

Yesterday I lost a dear friend. There are not enough words in the Cician language to convey the depth of my grief. I miss Marise. I know I will see her again in the Meadows when my time comes, but this is a meager consolation.

The funeral will take place the day after tomorrow and will last most of the day. Elias already ordered a full month of public mourning, but the mourning in my heart will last far longer. He was so stoic when he made the announcement. How can he remain so calm, when I *cry every hour of the day? I wish I was as resilient as he is.*

ELIAS DIDN'T CRY when Marise died. Neither did he cry at her funerals, nor when he publicly announced his intent to marry again.

That he sought a new wife surprised no one. He had no heir and the right—the *obligation*, in truth—to find another bride to carry his future children. What surprised everyone was his intent to marry *you*.

"But I am your *sister*," you argued, dumbfounded by his proposal. How could he sit so casually on his throne and declare the unthinkable to you, and in front of his guards, no less? At least he had the decency not to make his heinous proposal in front of the entire court. "What about the law?"

"I am the king. I make the law. If I want to marry my sister, I will marry her."

You shook your head in disbelief. "Father would have never approved of it."

"Indeed, he never approved."

You opened your mouth to respond, but you froze. At last, after an uncomfortable silence, you pulled yourself from your stupor and asked, "What do you mean?"

"Do you really think I wanted to marry Marise?"

You let the question sink into your mind until you felt nauseous. "You wanted to marry me before," you stated blankly, realizing you had mistaken his mild reaction to Marise's death as resilience, when it had genuinely left him unmoved, for he had never loved her.

"I've *always* wanted to marry you, Cyrelle. Father wouldn't let me, so I married a woman he picked for me who was enough to my liking. But Father is dead now."

"What about Mother?" you asked pressingly.

"She has no power over me, nor does she have power over the laws."

It was true, but you still hoped his love for your mother would make him change his mind. "She will be heartbroken."

"Why would she? Her two children will marry the person they love the most."

You blinked. Despite his flaws, you loved your brother, but with a different love—and he was certainly not the person you loved the most. You never imagined kissing him like a lover, and the idea of intimacy with him repulsed you. Inbreeding also meant a higher risk of genetic diseases and displeased noble families, since it prevented others from marrying their children into the royal family. Your ancestors had made unions between siblings illegal for more than one reason.

As he approached you and put his hand on your cheek, you wished your father wasn't dead and would stand between you and Elias. Everything made sense now. Elias's unusually long and tight embraces that you mistook for a deep brotherly affection, and your father telling him to let you breathe. Elias's longing looks he should have cast at Marise, but that you often caught being cast upon you. Your father's eagerness to find you a suitable husband, and Elias's support when you pushed back against his recommendations. Elias hadn't been trying to protect you from a marriage you had no interest in. He only wanted to keep you for himself. *Did Mother know, too?* you wondered. No, she would have warned you. Your father must have kept this secret to himself, taking it to the grave to spare your mother from the hideous truth.

"What is your answer, Cyrelle?" he asked.

Your answer. *Do I really have a choice?* you silently asked yourself. You were a princess, but he was the king.

"I love you, Brother, but—"

"Then it's settled," he said. "We will announce the royal wedding and—"

"Wait!" you pleaded. "I need… time to think about it. It is not a hasty decision to make."

He frowned, and you guessed his frustration by the way he lifted his chin and stuck out his chest. "I see you are confused. Marise's loss still affects you. I know how close you two were. But believe me, she would have wanted the two of us to be happy. Why don't you hold a serening ritual for yourself, Cyrelle? It would help clear your mind."

You nodded slowly. The *No* you wanted to shout was impossible to say without angering him. What would he do if you refused? Elias was clever but irascible, and he reacted to opposition with cold and violent retribution. Would he unleash his temper on his own sister, whom he professed to love? He had done it before. You were fully aware of what he was capable of. Would he force you to marry him? He could, and you knew it.

"I will do that, yes," you answered, bowing your head respectfully so you could also hide the tears coming to your eyes.

Relieved to have an excuse to leave, you fled to your apartment and sat cross-legged on the floor in front of your serenity shrine. You weren't confused and had already made your decision, but a serening ritual still appealed to you.

You took a deep breath, ready to begin, when Marise's

words echoed in your mind. *Serenity kills your will.* Serenity felt delightful and brought peace to those you serened. It had brought peace to you in times of need, taming your inner demons, silencing your torments and your desire for vengeance, for violence, for anything unreasonable you had ardently coveted at times.

Nobody knew it except your precious diary-screen, but there had been moments when you had wished ill upon others. Cousins mocking your mother, the queen, for her modest origins and teasing you for them when you visited them as a child. They had played so many tricks on you, these cruel children who had grown up to be ruthless adults. Their false modesty when they bowed exaggeratedly in front of your father. How they asked him for favors, then insulted your mother behind his back and criticized him for marrying her instead of a noble. You had considered telling it all to your father and asking him to punish them, hopefully violently—which he might have done, for he would have done so much for his dear daughter—but a serening ritual brought you back to your senses, killing your desire to exact a needless vengeance for what was, after all, not worth such ire.

What if it killed your much-needed desire to escape a marriage with Elias?

You couldn't let that happen. So, you stood up and left the palace.

ON THE HIGHEST hill of Hyla, Cicia's capital, stood the Temple of Serenity. Its rules did not allow ships in the vicinity, not even yours or the king's, so you walked.

After climbing the three hundred steps leading to the temple, you entered and stopped at the altar of Zephis. The Old People used to revere the Goddess of Serenity under other names, under other skies, until they forgot her and her divine siblings and lost themselves in the cult of a false god pretending to be the only one in existence. But our civilization found Zephis and the others again, their essence the same as it had been for thousands of years. A name was just a name. Only the essence mattered.

You dropped to your knees and asked for the goddess's blessing absentmindedly, as you had done so many times. Thankfully, a simple blessing wouldn't bring you true serenity like a serening ritual would, so your will would remain intact while your humor would improve. You kept praying until the goddess's blessing filled your heart with soothing warmth, making you feel well enough to meet your mother. You rose and walked to the courtyard where the Serenitors and Serenitresses usually were enjoying some leisure time before the evening collective prayers.

You found your mother there among others who had, like her, vowed to dedicate their lives to Zephis after being trained in the serening arts. The High Priest was here, too. He welcomed you like a grandfather would welcome his granddaughter—which you were, in a way. As an orphan, your mother grew up in the temple. The Serenitors and Serenitresses were her only family until your father, then a young prince, fell madly in love with her while attending a serening ritual. She left for the palace after their wedding, only to come back as a widow, ready to take her vows.

"Something troubles you," the High Priest said.

"Yes, indeed."

"Sister Lilla," he said, referring to your mother, "will host a ritual for you if you can't attain serenity on your own."

"I am here to see my mother, but not for a serening ritual," you said, kindly but firmly, before turning to your mother. "Mother, I need to talk to you. In private."

She nodded, and together you walked back inside the temple to the Fountain of Whispers. Coral and pearls decorated the fountain in intricate, hypnotizing patterns meant to soothe the spirit of the people who struggled to attain serenity. Your mother lit a stick of sandalwood incense before kneeling on a blue cushion.

"Elias wants to marry me," you said, sitting next to her.

"So, this is true," she whispered, closing her eyes. "I couldn't believe it when word reached the temple."

Elias hadn't made his proposal in front of the entire court, but the guards present in the throne room had heard every word of it, which meant your brother didn't intend for the information to remain confidential until you gave your answer. You weren't surprised the news was already spreading like wildfire through reader-screens.

"You must reason with him," you said.

"You know I cannot do that. The vows I pronounced forbid me from interfering with public life."

"Public life," you said, a lump in your throat. "I am your daughter!"

"You are Cyrelle, princess of Cicia, and your brother is the king. This… unholy proposal is a royal matter, not one I am allowed to interfere with. If I served Ameris," she said, referring to the god overseeing all contracts and unions, including marriage, "I could argue with him. But I am not, and I am sure your brother has already found an ambitious priest willing to bend to his will and officiate the wedding to gain his favor, no matter what Ameris thinks of marital unions between siblings. The best I can do is advise you. If Elias comes, I could advise him, too, but I know he won't listen. When he has made up his mind, it's impossible to make him change it."

You exhaled softly. She was right, but you had still hoped she could, somehow, talk your brother out of it. "What should I do?"

"You can't say no to him. Not directly. He won't tolerate it, and Zephis knows what his retribution will be. One way or another, he will hurt you if you displease him."

"I know," you whispered, bringing your hand to your face. Your brother was close to you once, protecting you from the annoying cousins, teaching you how to play many games, taking you on your first excursions in the city, and behaving like a brother should behave. Caring and supportive. Things changed, and slowly but surely, he matured into an irascible young adult unable to accept any form of resistance, especially from his sister, who was also growing up and asserting herself. Your fond childhood memories of Elias were tainted by the first and only time he raised his hand to you, when he slapped you after you asked him to stop hurting his horse. He promised never to do it again and kept his word, but you still remembered the burning sensation on your cheek all the same. You had long hoped that as he grew older, his temperament would revert to his calmer self, but it had never happened, and now you doubted it ever would.

"But you can't say yes either," your mother continued. "You must refuse without antagonizing him."

"How?"

She paused, thinking. "A condition to your agreement," she finally said. "Ask him for something impossible. A nuptial gift that he'll feel compelled by his pride to give you, but that he won't be able to deliver despite his wealth and power."

It sounded like a good idea, but you didn't know what you could ask of Elias that he could not provide. The kingdom's wealth was immense, thanks to Celadon, a giant diastium-eating snake from the planet Phau. She was the last of her kind and lived in captivity in the Cician palace's serpentarium. Every month, Celadon shed an emerald-green skin a hundred times more potent than the raw diastium she fed on. Cicia used it to power its diastium engines, which meant the kingdom had no need for the production of its diastium mines and could sell the excess to other countries at a high price.

"Tell me, Mother, what I could ask of him."

"Ask him," she said after sitting silently for a few minutes, "for a suit as radiant as the sun. The suit should be as practical and resistant as any space suit, but of a beauty and radiance only the sun could possess. Tell him this would content your heart and make you willing to marry him."

"What if he succeeds?" you asked, your voice trembling.

"Trust me, he won't."

Upon hearing these reassuring words, you hugged your mother and returned to the palace. You found your brother in his apartment and immediately asked him for the suit as a condition for the wedding to happen.

"You know how I love spaceflight," you promptly said to justify yourself as you noticed his furrowed eyebrows. "Almost as much as Marise loved it."

"Yes," he snapped, "and look what it did to her."

"I know, Brother. I don't intend to travel across the galaxy on a racing ship like the *Starling*. I will use the *Lifebringer*," you said, referring to the royal Cician spaceship orbiting Therria that Elias used for interstellar travel. "If I am to become the new queen, I will need to visit our colonies often."

"We have plenty of regular space suits to keep you safe," he said. "Why do you need one that looks like the sun?"

You could have told him it was to please you and your taste for fashion, but you doubted it would be enough to convince him. You knew flattery would soothe him. "I will need a suit that will make my travels safe and easy, but that is also worthy of the queen of the greatest of all the kingdoms."

Cicia wasn't the greatest kingdom, if by greatest you meant the largest, the most influential, or the kingdom with the greatest fleet, but it surely was the wealthiest— and for Elias, money made up for everything else.

You cleared your throat and continued before he had a chance to argue. "You are a charismatic king, whose aura shines like a star in the night. I am but a mere princess raised to worship a goddess, not rule over a kingdom. I fear my own… character isn't what you need in a queen."

"Your character is just fine as it is," he said dismissively.

"No," you said, gulping, and you actually meant it. Regardless of your desire to avoid marrying your brother, you had never planned to become a queen. You were a shy princess who had never learned to speak in public or command a room. Surely your brother saw it too, and would agree you needed help to look more charismatic. "You need a queen as radiant as you are to rule by your side. Not the meek Serenitress that I am. A suit radiant like the sun will make me look as bright as you are."

"Very well," he said after a long pause during which you had to stifle the urge to continue your plea. "You will receive a suit radiant like the sun. A suit worthy of the queen of Cicia."

As relief washed over you, Elias pulled out his reader-screen and tasked his fleet commander and the best suit-maker of all Cicia to work on the impossible request.

"Are you sure they are capable of delivering such a suit?" you asked, hinting at the enormousness of the task.

"Of course," he said, putting down his device, not an ounce of doubt in his voice. "What I request, my subjects deliver. I have enough gold and means to pay for whatever is needed to get the work done."

Your heart sank as you realized your mother might have been wrong. His confidence didn't sound delusional. He knew the task was hard—otherwise, he wouldn't have asked two of the highest-ranking people to complete it— yet he didn't believe it to be impossible like you did. What if he actually succeeded?

You retreated to your apartment and spent the next day in a torpor from which you escaped only to lunch with your brother. He insisted on eating on the terrace over-looking the gardens. An intense heat plagued the city that day, but he had the parasols removed, only allowing you to wear a wide-brimmed hat to protect your fair skin from the sunbeams.

"We shall enjoy this glorious day under the radiance of our star," he said, obviously referring to your request from the previous day.

You ignored his remark and ate your meal in silence.

As the servants arrived with dessert, a brief shadow passed above you, then another one, and you looked up for the unexpected clouds. The others imitated you, and you all gasped—except for Elias—as there were no clouds in the sky. Instead, the sun was flickering like a pulsar in the night.

"Your Majesty, what is happening?" a visibly alarmed servant asked Elias before you could.

He replied languidly, "Nothing you should feel concerned about."

Within moments, the sun returned to its normal self, shining brightly above your head with a steady light.

You left the terrace with a knot in your stomach, unable to eat the lemon pie the palace chef had prepared for you. What you had seen felt wrong. Only a fool would believe it was a mere coincidence—and you weren't a fool. That's why you were dismayed but not surprised when the next day, Elias presented the suit to you.

It was made of gold-lamé woven from diastium fiber, also called diaston, the strongest and most expensive fiber in the galaxy, known for its ability to absorb and retain liquids and other substances. The suit-maker had infused the diaston with molten gold—and, Elias explained, *with the sun itself.*

"I had a piece of the sun harvested for that suit to be made, Cyrelle," he said calmly.

You touched the suit and felt a soft but terrifying warmth penetrate your skin.

"You can control it to emit as much light and warmth as you wish," he explained, showing you control buttons on the right sleeve of the suit. He hadn't forgotten that you were left-handed, and he'd ensured the suit would meet your every need.

"As much as the sun itself?" you asked defiantly.

"As much as the sun itself, if you wish. Though it would be a silly and dangerous thing to do, don't you think, Cyrelle?"

You nodded, unwilling to ask him to prove it here, now, and risk killing everyone in the palace. He had captured the essence of a star in a suit! To your distress, the suit truly was as radiant as the sun. Even had the diaston not been infused with the sun, the golden fabric and the hundreds of tiny diamonds that covered the suit were enough to dazzle everyone's eyes.

"I thank you for this gift, Brother," you said. "It is a suit worthy of a queen that will undoubtedly make me as radiant and charismatic as you are. I will give you my answer tomorrow morning at dawn, on the terrace where we enjoyed lunch yesterday."

Surprisingly, he didn't look upset at you for postponing your answer until the next morning. He had probably expected you to accept right after seeing the suit, but the way you spoke—so calmly, so confidently—must have convinced him you had made your decision already and delayed your answer only for the sake of form.

You put the suit on, ran to the temple, and found your mother. Upon seeing the brilliance of your attire, your mother covered her mouth with her hand, realizing she had been wrong to assume Elias couldn't move Meadows and Therria to deliver what you had asked for.

"This is lunacy," she said after you explained everything to her. "He must have spent millions of credits to get this suit made. And the sun. I can't believe he infused diaston with the sun."

"I can't believe it either, but this is true. What shall we do now, Mother?"

She took a moment to think, then said, "Ask him for another suit… as celestial as our moon. He can infuse diaston with the sun to make it as radiant as a star, but what is he going to infuse diaston with to make it celestial? Moon dust?"

You nodded. This time, it would work. He couldn't harvest the moon like he had harvested the sun. You thanked your mother and returned to the palace, where you locked yourself in your apartment until the next morning and readied your arguments to request one more suit. Elias wouldn't be pleased by another demand when he had already thought the first to be superfluous.

At dawn, you went to the terrace to give your answer to Elias.

He was already there, waiting for you. "I am listening," he said, not even wishing you a good morning.

"I have given a lot of thought to your proposal," you said. "I will accept it if you offer me another suit which—"

"Another suit? Wasn't the first one good enough?"

"It was perfect," you said, "but I fear I need more than looking radiant to be worthy of being your queen."

He sighed. "What, then?"

"I don't have your gravitas, Brother. Not only do you shine like a star in the night, but you also know how to influence others, how to *lead* them. I am a mere follower if I cannot assert my own influence. Think about how your counselors would react to my presence at the council. Will they listen to me? Will they think of me as a leader?"

This time, he didn't challenge your assessment of your own worth. Instead he asked, "And how shall another suit help you gain more *gravitas*? Isn't the first one good enough to achieve that goal?"

"The sun-suit is perfect to impress the masses," you said, carefully reciting your prepared speech, "but politicians and counselors need something more subtle. I want a suit as celestial as the moon."

He stared at you for a moment, visibly confused, before asking, "What does that even mean?"

You gestured toward the sky, where the pale moon still shone despite the sunrise. "Isn't she grandiose? Imagine if I looked like her. Your royal counselors and foreign diplomats would respect me if I had more gravitas."

Before he could ask more questions, you said you were confident he would honor your request, and you returned to your apartment. You learned later that, like last time,

Elias tasked his fleet commander and the suit-maker to work on your bizarre demand.

That same evening, Elias summoned you to the terrace for a late dinner. The moon was up in the sky again, and you stared at it as if it was about to burst in front of your eyes. But nothing happened to the moon—nothing that you could see from Therria, at least.

"She's magnificent," Elias said, looking at the moon, too. "No other astral body rivals her beauty. Not even the sun."

"That is very true," you said. Then you added, probing his confidence once more, "I wonder how someone could capture its majesty and power. It seems impossible to me."

"Impossible isn't Cician," he responded matter-of-factly, as if it was the most evident thing in the world.

You nodded, wondering what you were missing. At last, the servants brought a round cake covered in gray icing. You ate silently. Something was happening—something related to the suit, like what had happened to the sun—but nothing you could see with the naked eye. When you finished your slice of cake, you thanked your brother and went to the palace's observatory.

You found the place empty except for the king's astronomer, who was working with the biggest telescope. You didn't interrupt him and instead took one of the portable telescopes and went into the gardens. After adjusting the device, you peeked into the lens, searching the moon for something unusual. Different states had claimed parts of the surface as their colonies, and the roofs of their underground buildings were just visible. You focused on the Cician territory. The telescope wasn't powerful enough to show you every detail of what happened on the ground, but you could see enough.

Nothing was happening.

You were about to put away the telescope and bring it back to the observatory when you noticed a ship leaving the Cician outpost. You followed it for a few seconds to guess its trajectory. It was traveling to Therria. Was it the commander of the Cician fleet, coming back from a mission? Or a routine transit?

You lowered the telescope and sighed. You were too exhausted to investigate further. If your brother succeeded in making a suit as celestial as the moon, you would find out soon enough. So you went back to your apartment and fell into a sleep as heavy as a black hole.

THE NEXT DAY, you expected Elias to summon you to give you the new suit, but he didn't. Actually, he was nowhere to be found in the palace. You asked his closest counselor about his whereabouts, but the man didn't know where Elias was.

Another day passed without seeing Elias at the palace, and for a moment, you wondered if you and your mother had succeeded. The new request was too complicated. Perhaps he would spend weeks, if not months, working on it. With a bit of luck, his desire to marry you would fade away and he would give up. You wouldn't have to say no. The marriage would simply not happen. He would choose a new bride and everyone would forget about how, once upon a time, the king had wanted to marry his sister.

Bitter disappointment fell on you the following day when your companion Darie, your most faithful servant, woke you up with what she said was urgent news. Rumor had it that today, the king would give you a new suit, and it would be ten times more impressive than the last one.

The rumor was true. Shortly after breakfast, Elias summoned you and showed you a new suit made of silver-lamé woven from diaston. The diaston wasn't infused with anything but still used for its incredible strength and beauty. Above the portable life-support system sat a rounded white plate that would cover your sternum. *What is this thing?* you almost blurted, but you kept it to yourself.

"Put it on," Elias ordered, "then meet me outside near the pond."

Too stunned to argue, you obeyed and returned to your apartment to change into the new attire you had hoped never to receive. Once you were ready, you went to the pond.

"Why here?" you asked.

"So you can observe how the suit is as 'celestial' as the moon." He pointed at the white plate on your chest. "This is a gravity generator. A prototype I intended to have installed on the *Lifebringer*, but that I am offering to you, Cyrelle."

You flushed, ashamed at how a precious device aimed at simplifying spaceflight was being used to satisfy a bogus request you had made only to avoid the wedding.

"You see," he continued, "it required a bit more creativity this time to meet your demand. You said you wanted a suit as celestial as the moon because you want to be respected. You want to be as grandiose as she is. More… gravitas, per your own words. I had to understand what the moon means to us, on Therria, and to the people of our moon colony. How this *celestial* body influences our lives uniquely, and how I can infuse this influence into a suit that will make you grandiose, Cyrelle. Gravity was the answer, obviously."

He gestured toward a control button on the suit, explaining how it allowed the generation of artificial gravity.

As soon as you activated it, the suit pulled the water in the pond toward you like the moon pulled Therria's oceans. You immediately turned it off.

"Thanks to another device inside the left sleeve, you can focus the effect on a specific direction, so you don't pull everything around you. It's important if you increase the strength of the artificial gravity. You wouldn't want to be crushed, would you?"

You shook your head and whispered, "No, of course not."

"If my counselors aren't irresistibly drawn to you—literally—and ready to listen to every single word you say, I don't know what else they need."

"Thank you," you said, dazzled by both the elegance of the suit and its technology. You hated to admit it, because it meant Elias had succeeded, but you already felt more confident simply by wearing it. You could see yourself in the *Lifebringer*, traveling between stars and sharing your opinion on royal matters to counselors eager to nod at your every word. "This is a magnificent gift."

"This isn't all," Elias said. "You see that other controller? It will make you truly *celestial*." He took your arm, making you shiver, and adjusted the control button. Then he said firmly, "Jump."

"What does it—"

"Jump," he repeated.

You swallowed hard and obeyed. As soon as you left the ground, you gasped. You were rising in the air as if you weighed nothing.

"Elias!" you shouted, but after only a couple of seconds, you fell down gently.

"The moon's gravity," he said.

"I know," you said after touching the ground. "I have been on the moon." The experience had still startled you, and you turned off the controller so you wouldn't repeat it inadvertently.

"You can replicate the gravity of many planets and moons. Not just our moon's."

"This is incredible," you said, half impressed, half terrified.

He looked you in the eye and whispered, "As celestial as the moon."

You knew what it meant. You couldn't deny the suit was exactly as you had demanded. Actually more than you had expected. How did the gravity generator work? And how could it affect the planet's gravity for its wearer only, allowing you to jump as if you were on the moon? Whatever technology he'd used, Elias must have spent a fortune on it. And it was only a prototype.

"As celestial as the moon," you said, nodding.

"Then I guess I will see you tomorrow morning to hear your answer? Unless you are ready to speak your mind already, Cyrelle."

"I—" you started, unsure of what to say next.

You couldn't say yes, but you couldn't say no either. An idea inspired by your mother sparkled in your mind, and this time, you knew he couldn't satisfy your request.

"Good things always come in threes," you said. "I require another gift. Give me a suit as inevitable as time."

Elias's eyes opened wide, but only for an instant. Then he said, "Is this becoming some sort of game, Cyrelle? If that is the case, you ought to know it isn't amusing."

"It is not," you said. "How could I be the queen of a country without mastering its biggest asset? Our economy is based on diastium. We have built our kingdom's wealth on it. We control space travel, which means we control time, Brother. Give me a suit that will make me the unquestionable master of time." After a brief pause during which you stared at him, looking for a reaction, you added, "This is the very last gift I require. After that, I believe I will be capable of ruling by your side. My heart will be contented."

Surely your brother couldn't deliver a suit capable of controlling time itself. Even diastium didn't actually control it. Once converted into fuel, diastium allows spaceships to open wormholes, curving the fabric of spacetime, but it doesn't allow you to travel back and forth in time. This request was truly impossible.

Elias mumbled something inaudible, sending another shiver down your spine as you worried your request had been too daring, but to your surprise, he didn't argue. "So be it. Last gift."

"Nothing you cannot deliver," you said, a hint of defiance in your voice.

He nodded confidently and said, "Nothing I cannot deliver indeed. You shall have a suit as inevitable as time."

"Thank you," you said, before going back to your apartment, a sensation of oppression filling your chest. It was your last chance to dodge this unwanted union, and so far, Elias had delivered everything that had seemed impossible. Hopefully this would be it, but you couldn't ignore the dread growing inside you, as if your inevitable doom was approaching.

You sent your companion and the other servants away, asking them to leave you alone for the rest of the day. Once you were sure no one could hear you, you let the tears come to your eyes and cried until you couldn't anymore.

A WEEK PASSED. Several times, the temptation to serene yourself came close to overwhelming you, but you remembered Marise's words. You needed to keep your will strong. Elias had already almost broken it when he gave you the moon-suit.

Each passing day should have made you more hopeful, but you could feel what was coming. Eventually, Elias would summon you and give you what you had asked for—*again*.

As a second week passed, you hoped again. Your plan finally worked. Your previous requests had failed to prevent the marriage only because you had underestimated the kingdom's wealth and Elias's determination to marry you. What sounded impossible to you was a simple matter of money for Elias. Harvesting the sun and infusing it into diaston, or implementing a groundbreaking gravity generator inside a suit... nothing credits couldn't buy. But time? What could he possibly possess to make a time-suit? Even all the diastium in the universe couldn't control time.

Councils kept Elias busy, and he regularly invited you for lunch or dinner. He never mentioned your latest request, even indirectly. He talked about politics, about the colonies, about Zephis and other gods and goddesses, asking for your advice when you least expected it, but never mentioned the suit, time, or the wedding itself.

But you soon found out that Elias had let your hope grow only to better kill it when, the third week coming to its end, he summoned you to the throne room along with his fleet commander and the suit-maker. The two men, who usually wore their hair short like Elias, had grown long manes. There he showed you a new suit made entirely of black diaston.

"You wanted a suit that would make you the master of time like our country is," Elias said. "But as you formulated it in your initial request, time is inevitable. We cannot turn it back, nor can we stop it. We can only go forward. Which is why your request sounded truly impossible to me at first. But impossible isn't Cician, is it? I gave it more thought, and I remembered that while time is inevitable, it is also relative."

Your eyes opened wide as he explained how his fleet commander had traveled into the depths of space to harvest a black hole so the suit-maker could infuse the diaston with it. But that wasn't all. On Elias's orders, the two men had tested the suit on themselves to prove its efficacy.

"You can't escape time," Elias said, "but with this suit, you can choose how fast it passes relative to those around you. You can live an hour when the rest of us experience only a minute. If this doesn't make you the master of time, I don't know what will."

The fleet commander and the suit-maker gave you imploring looks that made your heart sink. They had given everything they had to satisfy their king, and their fate was now in your hands. Would you accept the suit, and with it, agree to marry your brother? Or would you have their lives destroyed by refusing the gift?

A lump in your throat, you sealed your fate. "I thank you, Brother"—you turned to the fleet commander and the suit-maker—"and you, sirs, for making my wish a reality."

Elias nodded, then dismissed the two men. They whispered their thanks to you and swiftly left the throne room, a weight off their shoulders. You wanted to follow them and leave, too, but Elias was looking at you impatiently. He wanted your answer now. You pressed your lips together in a thin line, unable to say another word.

He approached you and said, his voice flat, "I granted each of your requests. A suit for each of the qualities you thought you didn't possess. You will be a queen worthy of

Cicia. I have made it possible. I have proven my love."

"You did," you said, though you disagreed with the latter statement. All he had proven was his determination to force you into an unwanted union. Because, despite all your excuses about being a so-called meek princess, you couldn't believe Elias didn't know how you felt about marrying him. He must have sensed your reluctance, disguised behind requests for seemingly impossible gifts.

"You said it would be the last gift. That if I gave it to you, your heart would be contented."

You looked at the suit, amazed by its technology and despairing that Elias had succeeded at creating it. "My heart is contented." You paused, weighing your next words carefully. Both yes and no were unsayable. So, instead, you put your hand on your heart and added, "I wish to visit the temple to pray to Zephis and get the blessing of the High Priest before any proceedings."

He sighed before saying, "As you wish. But the wedding will happen with or without his blessing. The High Priest has no say in this matter. He doesn't serve Ameris, and a priestess of the Temple of Accords has already approved my request and will officiate our wedding."

You clenched your fists, not surprised at his ability to manipulate a priestess into blessing a union her own god disapproved of. Surely, Elias had promised to support her so she would become the next High Priestess of her temple. Elias knew how to use ambitious people to his own advantage.

"I know," you said, "but it would still please me to ask for his blessing. And Zephis's wisdom will guide me into this next chapter of my life."

Elias gave you a smile you hadn't expected. "Your piety is always an inspiration, Cyrelle. Perhaps I should imitate you. Visit the Temple of Fortune, ask the High Priestess for her blessing, and pray to Eterion for a fruitful union."

"You should do that, Brother," you said. Your father and his ancestors had been followers of Eterion since your dynasty had come into power. Eterion's adepts—Fortuners, they called themselves—invoked the god in rituals, asking for abundance, prosperity, and good fortune. According to a bedtime story your late father used to tell you, he had found Celadon after invoking Eterion for three days without eating or sleeping.

You ran to the temple without looking back. You climbed the stairs four at a time and came face-to-face with your mother.

"I've been waiting for you," she said.

"Elias—"

"I know. He gave you two more suits, and you have no choice but to accept his proposal. Saying no now would drive him mad."

"I know. He could kill me," you said, squeezing her hands. "But I can't accept his proposal either."

She raised an eyebrow. "My son will not murder my daughter, and he won't marry her either. We will find a solution."

You nodded, then said hesitantly, "I should take my vows and join the temple." It was the only path left to avoid marrying Elias. One you had never imagined taking.

"No," she said. "It isn't a life for you."

"I am already a Serenitress," you argued. "I know how to serene myself and other people, how to lead rituals—"

"This is not the same."

"But—"

"One does not take their vows before they've lived in the temple for at least three years. It's a life of solitude and prayer. We don't travel across space. We don't explore. I know you, daughter. You wouldn't be happy."

"But it's my only way out of this marriage!"

"It is *not*," she said, grabbing you by the elbow. She took you inside the temple. "Also, how do you think Elias would react if we let you become a priestess? We rely on taxes that he has the power to reassign to another temple. The donations of our followers wouldn't be enough. Your brother would have us starve until we release you from your obligations."

You lowered your gaze. She was right. Taking your vows would only bring trouble to the temple.

"Elias has satisfied your requests because of his wealth and an absurd determination to spend it outrageously," your mother said as she sat in front of the Fountain of Whispers. She clasped her hands in her lap. "Ask him to kill Celadon and give you her skin as proof. If he can sacrifice half of the kingdom's wealth to meet your demands, he cannot sacrifice what makes his wealth possible. All his Fortuner tricks won't make up for Celadon's loss."

"Celadon," you whispered.

"The larger she grows, the richer the kingdom is. She was already taking up a quarter of the Royal Serpentarium when I left the palace."

"But I told him the time-suit would be the last gift I asked for," you said. "If I ask him for one more gift, he will be furious."

"Not as a gift. As a divine sacrifice. Tell him you had a vision of Zephis in which she asked for the snake to die before you could marry him. To bring serenity to the kingdom. Because Celadon is growing too big and be-coming dangerous. Whatever he'll believe, as long as he understands that it's a nonnegotiable condition for you to enter a marriage with him."

"But I can't lie about what a goddess asks me!" you said quickly, uncomfortable with your mother's suggestion. "Zephis hasn't—"

"Do you want to prevent this wedding from happening or not?"

You gulped, still uneasy. "What if he does it? What if he kills poor Celadon?" The giant snake looked awfully scary, but she was a gentle beast whose mind was lost in memories of Phau. Several times, you had serened her after stressful sloughings and had felt sorry for her. She missed the lair she had carved inside a rocky diastium-rich plateau. She missed the grass brushing her skin and the sun warming her scales and the wind blowing sand over her sleek body. Perhaps Celadon had once wanted to break away from her prison, but over the decades, she had fallen into a melancholic dreamlike state from which she escaped only to shed her precious skin and eat.

"The livelihood of the kingdom depends on Celadon. Without her, Elias will have to use the production of his mines to power the diastium engines and stop selling it to other states, or give up interstellar travel, which would affect the outer colonies that rely on regular supply shipments for their survival. Believe me. He won't kill her."

You nodded. It would work. It had to work. Elias's determination to marry you was strong, but you knew he valued the kingdom's wealth—and by extension, his own—more than anything else. Should he accept the slaughter of Celadon, all hope would be lost. You would either give in to the wedding or choose to follow Celadon and Marise in their eternal sleep.

You shivered. Before today, you had never considered that latter path, but it now seemed appealing. Everything would be easier. Your spirit would join the gods in the Meadows. Perhaps Zephis would have a special place for you in her domain.

"You're crying," your mother said.

Tears you hadn't known you were holding rolled down your cheeks, and you whispered, "I don't feel well, Mother."

"We should hold a ritual together to soothe you," she said, gently putting her hand on your shoulder.

"No," you said. "I—I need to keep my will strong if I am to refuse this union."

She frowned and gave you a surprised look. You expected her to scold you, but she smiled and said, "Do you remember your training, Cyrelle? When you learned to clear your mind and ignore all the troubles life had cast upon you."

"Yes, I remember."

"Occasionally, you would struggle and delve into a confusing state where your mind focused on a bad memory, preventing you from accomplishing the ritual. I want you to do that again. I want you to hold onto your negative feelings toward your brother and his proposal. But, instead of drowning in them and failing the ritual, I want you to leverage your determination to refuse his demands to serene the rest of yourself that needs it."

"But," you said, flinching, "this is not—"

"Do you think all Serenitors and Serenitresses attain serenity every time they host a ritual?"

"This is different. I would do it on purpose. This is *corruption*. You know how terrible the consequences can be!"

"I know very well. I have warned you myself, but I know what I am doing, Cyrelle. Trust me."

You pressed your lips into a thin line, pondering your

mother's assertion. The faith you had always placed in her was now damaged by the past three failures to counter Elias's desires. Did your mother truly know what she was doing? Would Elias refuse to kill Celadon? Would a corrupted ritual ease your mind? You weren't sure of anything anymore.

"What about Zephis? Even if you don't harm me, she won't approve," you argued.

"Zephis will forgive us for corrupting the ritual," your mother answered confidently. "Everything we're doing, we're doing to protect your virtue. You must not marry your brother, no matter the cost, no matter the hardships, no matter how many gods we offend. When your virtue prevails, they'll understand."

You sighed. Despite your doubts, you knew your mother was right. You had to dodge this union, and you needed to be in the right state of mind to do so. If she said she knew what she was doing, who were you to argue? She wasn't only your mother. She was a devout priestess and Serenitress with decades of experiences you didn't have.

She wiped the tears from your face and took your hand. "Cyrelle, close your eyes and listen to my voice. I will guide you."

You nodded and did as she said. Squeezing your mother's hand to establish a strong spirit-bond, you inhaled deeply and prepared yourself for the ritual. Admittedly, you were relieved. You hadn't serened yourself for weeks and had let false hopes and despair grow inside your heart, bringing you to the verge of self-destruction. You needed to keep your will strong, but you also needed comfort.

Following the soft and confident voice of your mother, you let her mind reach yours and sort through your deepest fears. If she saw your recent thoughts about giving up on life, she didn't mention it.

"Think about your brother's proposal and hold on to that memory. Hold on to the disgust and the anger you felt when you heard his confession."

Your heartbeat and your respiration quickened at once as the uncomfortable feelings invaded your mind, but before they could overwhelm you, your mother steadied your thoughts. Her mind soothed yours and her voice kept guiding you until, at last, you felt as if a heavy burden had left your shoulders.

"Excellent," she said. "You can open your eyes now."

You felt dirty for allowing yourself to corrupt the ritual, but it also felt good. Although you had not reached true serenity, your mind was tranquil. The death wishes were gone, and your willingness to face your brother was intact. You wondered, though, what would have happened if your mother had not seized control over your mind—or worse, if she had reinforced your negative feelings. You had trained so hard to master the arts of serenity. You were constantly warned of the dangers of botched rituals: increased anxiety, panic attacks, and even, in the worst cases, hallucinations and psychosis. Could you have poisoned your own mind, losing yourself in a permanent state of anger or terror?

Regardless, you felt better, and your resolve was unchanged—stronger, actually. Only that mattered. You had a wedding to avoid, and a truly impossible request for your brother. Celadon would live, and your brother's determination would die, killed by his greed.

FOURTHDAY 11 GELOIS 1496 AE
HYLA, KINGDOM OF CICIA, THERRIA

Mother did something both terrible and wonderful today. She showed me corrupting the serening ritual doesn't always lead to terrible consequences. She relieved my distress, but she took immense risks doing so. There is a reason we are warned against straying from the temple's teachings.

Despite the risks, what Mother did was worth it. I wish she had been there when I told Elias I wanted him to kill Celadon! The stupefaction on his face made him look like he had been struck by lightning. I don't know if he was shocked by the request or by the way I asked it.

Thanks to Mother, today I didn't need to wear a suit to radiate confidence.

"HAVE YOU LOST your mind?" Elias shouted after you stated your request.

"On the contrary," you said. "My mind has never been clearer. I prayed to Zephis and—"

"To the Meadows with Zephis!"

"Brother!" you said, raising your voice. "How can you blaspheme so brazenly?" You bit your lip, silently ashamed to be accusing Elias of blasphemy when you were lying about Zephis's request.

"I follow Eterion, and he *blessed* our family with Celadon."

"Things have changed," you argued. "And we must obey all the gods, not only the one you serve."

He clicked his tongue. He knew you were right. Disobeying a divine order from any deity was a great sin. "What has changed?"

"Celadon has grown too big. She is becoming dangerous. Zephis showed me a vision of Celadon destroying the palace and eating us in our own marital bed. I will marry you, but there will be no ceremony until you put an end to this threat."

He didn't answer. Instead, he looked at you placidly, visibly thinking. Even though there was no spirit-bond between you at that moment, you could easily guess what thoughts raced through his mind. He had already spent an inordinate amount of money from the royal reserve to satisfy your demands, and he couldn't afford to lose Celadon. It was too much. A blow from which he wouldn't recover. Yet the story of your vision troubled him.

"I will need time to think about it," he said at last. "To quote your own words, it's not a hasty decision to make."

You gave him a smug smile and said, "Take all the time you need."

IT TOOK A month for Elias to make up his mind. During that time, he spent hours praying at his shrine to Eterion and left the palace every day to consult the High Priestess. He invited you sometimes, but you always politely declined, saying that your long prayers to Zephis exhausted you.

"Tell me if you get another vision," he often asked you,

"or if Zephis tells you something different."

Zephis didn't tell you anything at all, so it was with confidence that you walked into the throne room on the thirtieth day after you had made your demand. It was empty, except for Elias and a half dozen guards standing around him, ready to obey his commands. The serious look on his face comforted you and fortified your certitude. He was about to tell you he wouldn't kill Celadon. There would be no wedding.

"It wasn't an easy decision," he said, "but Eterion, once again, blessed our family."

He gestured to his guards, and two of them left the room. They came back carrying a machine shaped like a strongbox. Elias opened it and took out two large eggs. They were white with dark green patches, and you knew immediately who had laid them.

"How is it possible?" you asked. "She is the last of her kind."

A triumphant smile spread across Elias's face. "Parthenogenesis, if we are to believe our exobiologists. Or, according to the High Priestess, a gift from Eterion." He put the eggs back in the machine—an incubator. "Zephis was right to warn you, Sister. She must have known about Eterion's plans, and that it would make Celadon dangerous. You see, she would have surely become aggressive to protect her eggs. But worry no more."

He gestured to his guards again, and this time, the six of them left the throne room. You had to cover your mouth with your hands to not shout when they came back carrying Celadon's skin and dropped it at your feet.

You had seen Celadon's molted skin many times, but this was incomparable. In front of you was a thick, bloody hide reeking of death. She was dead. Dead because of you. You had lied about receiving a vision from Zephis, and Elias's god had answered by mocking you. Not only had Elias satisfied your awful demand, he had done so without having to sacrifice his wealth. Soon he would have two new snakes. It would take time for them to grow and shed large pieces of skin, but it would only be a matter of months. Nothing the kingdom couldn't endure.

"Celadon is no more," Elias said. "She won't threaten us, and soon her children will serve the kingdom."

You swallowed hard, holding back the tears that wanted to flow from your eyes, and said, "We are truly blessed." You realized your voice was shaking, so you excused yourself, promising to come back quickly.

The sound of your heels clattering against the marble floor filled the air as you dashed to your apartment. You slammed the door behind you, rushed to your serenity shrine, and fixed Zephis's statuette with imploring eyes.

"Forgive me," you whispered to the goddess, throwing yourself to your knees. "I never wanted Celadon to die. She was innocent. I lied to save myself, but I lied in your name and at her expense."

The statuette silently stared back at you.

"Tell me what I can do to redeem myself. I will do anything, even marry"—you choked on your words—"even marry my brother if that is the price to pay."

But nothing happened. Was Zephis ignoring you? Was she punishing you by refusing to answer when you needed her the most? Or did she expect something else from you?

Yes, that was it. Marrying your brother wouldn't bring Celadon back. She was gone, her spirit on its way to Phau's Golden Isles—the equivalent of Therria's Meadows. You exhaled loudly, trying to focus. What could you do now that Celadon was gone? What was left to repair?

The eggs. Celadon's children. If Elias kept them as he

intended to, they would live in a cage their entire lives. You could spare them from what their mother endured.

"I will release Celadon's children to the wilderness," you said, and you sensed something changing in the air. Yes, that was it. "I will care for them. I will show them visions of Phau, I will—"

You didn't finish your sentence because the statuette's eyes shone and pierced your mind, sending you a vision—an *actual* vision this time. Your entire body shook, and you fell on the floor, convulsing. Celadon's terrifying golden eyes looked at you as if they could see your very spirit.

I am so sorry, Celadon, you thought, expecting the vision to swallow you whole. But the golden eyes disappeared, and the Temple of Serenity replaced them. Celadon's skin was lying on the floor in the courtyard. Did Zephis want you to take the skin to her temple? An offering, perhaps? Or a ritual to serene the snake's spirit? You didn't have time to think more about it because another vision appeared, and this time, it took you a moment to recognize the place.

Zephis was sending you a vision of an immense savanna bordered by high plateaus—you had been there only once in your life, but you still recognized the New Zankia region on Phau, not far from the Cician colony in which you had spent countless vacations in your life. It wasn't only a vision; the goddess was triggering all your senses, controlling your mind and tricking it to make you believe you were breathing the savanna's dust and sensing Phau's blazing sun on your skin. Did she want you to go there? Probably, you told yourself. Otherwise, why would she make you sense the place as if you had already arrived?

The vision stopped before you could get any answers. Staggering to get up, you realized someone was knocking at the door of your apartment. How long had you been gone from the throne room? Probably only a few minutes, but these visions had felt like they'd taken hours.

"I'm coming," you said.

You opened the door.

In the corridor was your companion. "His Majesty sent me to look for you," she said. "Are you all right, ma'am?"

"Yes, Darie," you lied. You hadn't looked in a mirror, but you knew your eyes were puffy and your hair a complete mess, and that wasn't accounting for your mind's unrest. "Let's go back to the throne room."

Celadon's skin was still on the floor, exactly where the guards had left it.

You took a moment to regain your composure and said, "Forgive my brief absence, brother. I had to reconvene with Zephis, to tell her that Celadon wasn't a threat anymore. She actually gave me another vision. She wants me to take Celadon's skin to the Temple of Serenity, so we can host a ritual to serene her spirit. We wouldn't want her to haunt us on our wedding day." You paused, searching for a reaction in your brother's eyes, but he kept looking at you patiently. "I will need help from the guards carrying it."

"Of course," he said at last, gesturing to his guards. "Escort Princess Cyrelle to the temple."

The men picked up the skin again and walked toward the exit. You moved to follow them, but you stopped and turned to your brother.

Looking him in the eyes, you asked, "Did she suffer?"

"Who?"

"Celadon. She may have become a dangerous beast, but in the end, she would have just been a mother defending her offspring like all good mothers do." You didn't know if this was true. Celadon had been so gentle that she would have surely let you approach the eggs and serene her future babies in the shell. "Did she suffer when she died?"

"No," he whispered, and while it didn't make you forgive him, you knew he was sincere.

THE TEMPLE'S PRIESTS gasped when the guards dropped Celadon's skin in the courtyard. Your mother, who must have heard the commotion, rushed outside. She stopped before you, her right hand covering her mouth and her left raised to her side, as if to tell others everything was under control.

She thanked the guards and sent them back to the palace. Before leaving, they bowed respectfully. She had renounced her place in the royal family when she took her vows, but she was still the queen mother in everyone's mind.

"For the love of Zephis, what is going on?" she whispered in your ear.

"Isn't it obvious?" you whispered back, frowning. "He did it. It's Celadon's skin. Our plan didn't work."

"I see that. But why did you bring it *here*?"

"Zephis told me to. I had a vision. A real one, this time, in my shrine at the palace."

She stifled a gasp. "Is this true?"

You nodded. "But I don't know why she wanted me to bring it here." You explained everything—the eggs, the vision, how you had to redeem yourself for Celadon's death.

"It's my fault," your mother said at last. "It was my idea. That's why Zephis sent you this vision. She wants *me* to atone for my sin, too."

"You tried to help me do the right thing, remember? You

said the gods would understand."

She shook her head. "But we failed. Celadon is dead, and you will marry your brother if we can't find another way to prevent it. I accomplished nothing. Worse, Eterion humiliated us, and by extension, Zephis."

You took her by the shoulders and said, "If I can't take my vows, and everything else has failed, then I should flee."

She stared at you silently for a moment, then looked at Celadon's skin. You didn't need to establish a spirit-bond to know what she was thinking. The way she moved her eyes and twisted her lips almost imperceptibly: She agreed with you and was coming up with an escape plan.

"You're right," she said in a grave tone, "and I will help you. But we must do it when Elias can't notice." She glanced at her fellows, who were busy examining Celadon's skin and whispering among themselves, but still within earshot. She pulled you away. "Tell Elias to proceed with the wedding, but make sure he plans a grand ceremony that will take at least a week to prepare. I will need time."

"Time for what?"

"Time to have a suit-maker secretly craft a suit and a mask out of Celadon's skin." You opened your mouth to protest, but she put her fingers on your lips. "It will make an admirable disguise. You are Cyrelle, princess of Cicia. Do you think you can hide from your brother if you show your face everywhere you go and wear royal attire? Of course not."

She was right. Everybody would recognize you, and not just in Cicia, not just on Therria. Unless you made your new home on a barren planet—where you wouldn't last long, since you hadn't trained to survive in the wilderness like a colonist—you were condemned to take a new identity and blend into a crowd where Elias would never think to look for you. Thankfully, you knew exactly where to go.

"I will disguise myself and go to Phau," you told your mother. "It's the perfect hideout, and taking Celadon's children there will allow me to follow Zephis's demand."

"A wise choice," she replied, nodding. "I won't say a word, even if he forces another Serenitor to explore my spirit. I swear it to Zephis, I will resist as much as I can if he dares do such a terrible thing. And I won't know exactly where you are, anyway. Phau is a big planet, and the New Zankia region spans multiple colonies." She paused, letting out a sigh. "Be prepared. Pack the minimum. Be discreet and don't let Darie see you."

You considered arguing that your companion was trustworthy and wouldn't tell Elias, but you couldn't be certain. Darie served you, but he was the king, after all.

"On the day of the wedding, you will remain in your apartment and, per tradition, Elias won't be allowed to see you. As for everyone else, they'll be busy finishing preparations for the ceremony and welcoming the guests. This will be your window of opportunity. I will visit you—as is expected from the bride's mother—and will bring the new suit and other things to help with your escape. Then I will visit Elias, as the—" She pursed her lips. "As the groom's mother is expected to do too. I'll divert his attention long enough so that you can discreetly go to the ship hangar and leave."

"I will be ready," you said, knowing exactly what ship to use. You would fly in the *Starling*, Marise's racing ship. No other ship in the palace matched its speed, and by the time Elias ordered your pursuit, you would have already gone through a wormhole to a place only known to yourself.

Your mother lowered her gaze, then looked at Celadon's skin again. "Before I have it taken to a suit-maker, we should hold a serening ritual like you told Elias. This is the least we can do for Celadon's spirit."

You nodded. Your mother gestured to the others to join you, and they formed a circle around what remained of Celadon. The ritual normally required the entire body of the deceased, but you didn't know what Elias had done with Celadon's flesh. The skin would have to be enough for Zephis to find and bless Celadon's spirit.

Your mother began the prayer, and soon you and the others joined her in unison, asking the goddess to relieve Celadon from her worldly worries and bless her with the serenity the living and the dead all aspired to achieve. Taking the lead after your mother discreetly nodded at you, you asked Zephis to help Celadon's spirit travel through the universe to Phau's Golden Isles, where she would forever rest in peace.

As you finished your prayer, you placed your hands on the part of the skin that used to cover Celadon's head, flinching at the coldness of the smooth scales. Then you whispered, "I will look after your children, Celadon. I promise."

A vision of Celadon's eyes filled your mind once again. Her spirit saw yours and knew that you would do anything to keep your promise. You saw her spirit, too. Celadon had found the path to the Golden Isles. She was ready for her last journey.

YOUR COMPANION WAS helping you get dressed when someone knocked on the door. She rushed to open it.

"Your Royal Highness," she exclaimed when your mother entered.

"You know I go by Sister Lilla now, Darie."

Your companion knew it like everyone else, but she had served your mother when she was the queen consort before serving you. Old habits died hard.

"I wish you would visit us more often, ma'am."

Your mother gave her a faint smile. "A Serenitress serving Zephis in her temple has no business in a royal palace. Only a personal duty can bring me here. This is why I've come today, for that matter. Not as the queen mother or as a priestess, but as the mother of the bride." *And of the groom*, you almost heard her think, but she had the decency not to say it out loud.

"Of course, ma'am. You wouldn't miss your daughter's wedding."

"I wouldn't miss it," she said softly, almost whispering, "for anything in the galaxy." Then she straightened up and added, her voice gentle but firm, "I will take it from here, Darie. We'll call you if we need your assistance."

"Absolutely, ma'am. I'll go help with other preparations until you call me," she said, before walking away and closing the door behind her.

Your mother put her ear against the door to listen for Darie's footsteps, and then she locked it.

"There's nobody else, right?" she asked, glancing at the door on the other side of the room that led to the rest of your apartment.

"No," you said. "It's only us."

"Good. Your things are ready?"

You nodded before dashing to your dressing table. Next to it was the red rounded pouf you sat on when your companion combed your hair. It had a storage compartment nobody ever opened—yourself included until yesterday, when you'd put your travel bag inside it.

"I packed the minimum," you told her. "Credits on a card unlinked to my accounts. Clothing as unremarkable as I could find from my wardrobe. Survival rations. The ship I will take also has supplies inside already." You noticed your mother had come empty-handed, and she didn't carry a backpack. "Where is the suit?"

She smiled and rolled up her left sleeve to reveal a device shaped like a vambrace wrapped around her wrist and forearm. She opened a small compartment at the top and took out a green marble.

"Is it—"

"My portable miniaturizer, yes. A gift from your father, that he inherited from his mother. I've always intended to give it to you in my old age. Given the circumstances, I believe you should have it now."

She placed the green marble on the floor and pointed at it with her miniaturizer. She pressed a button on the device, and the green marble turned into a green suit. You gasped, incredulous. You had already seen her use her miniaturizer in the past, but the device still impressed you, especially because of how small it was. Such technology encapsulated in a tiny device was as miraculous as the suits Elias had gifted you. The only other miniaturizer in the kingdom you knew about was as big as the *Starling* and belonged to the Cician merchant fleet, which used it to manage the sizeable amount of diastium transported by each of its ships. Barely a handful of other miniaturizing devices existed in the galaxy, all belonging to foreign rulers or rich businessmen.

You picked up the green suit and admired the work of the suit-maker your mother had hired. Unlike your three other suits, it wasn't made of diaston, a man-made fiber, but the suit was stunning all the same. It was beautiful, but also terrifying, like Celadon herself. The glossy scales covered the suit in vivid patterns of emerald and viridian greens. The color of diastium itself, absorbed and concentrated in Celadon's very skin.

"Try it," your mother said.

You took off the white dress you wore and put the suit on. It fit perfectly.

"Now, put this on your face."

She took something out of her pocket and presented it to you. A mask made with Celadon's smallest scales. You applied it to your face, where it immediately adhered to your skin. It covered the lower half of your face, from nose to chin, and included a small voice-warping device.

Looking at your reflection, you said, a little queasy, "I look like Celadon in human form." As expected, your voice came out distorted. Deeper. *What have I done?* you wondered. *Celadon is dead by my fault, and now I wear her skin like a costume.* It was to hide yourself, you knew, but the distasteful feeling stuck nonetheless.

"I wouldn't recognize you if I didn't already know who you were," your mother said. "But let's put it back in the miniaturizer. We don't want anyone in the palace to see you wearing this attire. Even if they don't recognize you, they will make the connection eventually, and Elias will order every spy in the galaxy to look for a woman wearing a snake-suit."

You nodded, took everything off, and gave the suit to your mother so she could miniaturize it again. In your wardrobe, you found a plain brown tunic and white straight pants that you tucked into your boots. You tied a beige cloak around your shoulders, wondering if you should put the hood on.

"Not in the palace," your mother said, as if she had heard

your thoughts. "You don't want to be mistaken for a thief and be arrested by the guards." She removed the miniaturizer from her forearm and attached it to yours. "The storage compartment has five more slots. Go get your other suits and miniaturize them, too."

"Why? I won't be able to wear them in public. Some people have seen the suits and know they are mine."

"Yes, but their power is immense. You may need to use them at some point."

She was right. Who knew what challenges would obstruct your journey? The snake-suit was perfect to hide your identity, but the other suits possessed advanced technology that could prove useful. You could trade the diaston alone for a small fortune, should you find yourself in need of credits.

Going back to your wardrobe, you miniaturized the suits one by one, then put the golden, silver, and black marbles into the storage compartment. You had two slots left, and you knew exactly what you would use them for: Celadon's eggs.

Once you were done, you went back to your mother and grabbed your travel bag.

"One more thing," she said. She plucked the tiara from your head and hid it inside the pouf. You were so used to wearing it that you had forgotten. "We should also cut your hair."

"No," you said. "Not this." You agreed to wear a snake-suit and to renounce your name, the palace, and life on Therria, but you wouldn't cut your hair. If you had to keep one thing from your past life, that would be it. Your long, beautiful auburn hair.

Your mother didn't argue. Although you refused to cut your hair, you still tied it into a bun. You usually wore your hair loose, so it would, at least, make you harder to recognize.

You were ready.

"I will go to Elias's apartment now," your mother said as she moved toward the door. "Be quick."

You nodded. You would go fast, moving as a shadow through the palace's lengthy corridors that you knew like the back of your hand, and not only because of your light and quick pace. Your mother was right about the suits possessing immense powers, and her words had just given you an idea. With the time-suit, Elias had given you the means to escape the palace in the literal blink of an eye.

"Mother," you whispered. She stopped, her hand already on the door handle. "Will I ever see you again?"

When she turned toward you, you couldn't help but notice how wet her eyes were. She opened her mouth to answer, but nothing came out. You hoped to see her again, but deep down, you knew. If you ever crossed paths in the future, it would mean you had failed. It would mean Elias had found you. Even if you hid long enough for Elias to grow impatient and find another bride, he would never forgive your betrayal. He could force you to marry him despite already having another wife. He didn't care for the laws his ancestors had made, and he could break the one that limited men and women to one spouse, too.

In silence, you hugged each other for the last time.

"Farewell, my sweet daughter," she said as she opened the door. "May you find serenity at the end of the long journey that awaits you."

"Farewell, Mother."

Then she was gone. The parting words left a bitter taste in your mouth, but you couldn't break down and cry now. Not while you were still on Therria. You would allow yourself to mourn your loss in the depths of space.

Quickly, you went back to your dressing table and took out the two glass eggs you had bought from a glassmaker a couple of days ago. They were mostly white, with greenish-brown spots differing significantly from the dark green patches covering Celadon's eggs, but it would fool the serpentarium workers until they opened the incubator for a closer inspection.

You took the black marble out of the miniaturizer's storage compartment and restored the time-suit to its regular size. Hastily, you took off your cloak and put the suit on over your plain clothes, which were thin enough to fit under the thick diaston. Observing yourself in your full-length mirror, covered in a diaston so black it looked like it absorbed all light into it, you swallowed as you realized it was the last time you were standing in your apartment. You tied the cloak over the suit and did your best to hide it under the beige fabric, just in case someone saw you and recognized the time-suit despite your speed. Then, without looking back, you placed the glass eggs in your travel bag, and you left your apartment and everything that made you a princess behind.

NO ONE SAW you as you slipped into the serpentarium. In your time-suit, one hour was a mere minute to others. You could have even made it a second, but it was your first time using the time-suit's abilities, and you didn't want to push it to its limit for fear of being swallowed by your own black hole–infused suit. Not that Elias had told you that could happen, but you preferred to avoid tempting fate.

Before switching Celadon's eggs with their glass

replicas, you checked the parameters of the incubator—
the temperature, in particular. Cician exobiologists had
studied Phau's similar native snake-like creatures for decades
and drawn conclusions about Celadon's species and her
needs. Their findings on how to care for the eggs would
ensure you didn't kill Celadon's children before they could
break out of their shell.

Then you miniaturized the eggs and stored the two white-
and-green marbles in the remaining slots of your storage
compartment. The eggs would be safe in your miniaturizer.
Suspended in stasis, their development would halt, but
wouldn't be compromised. As soon as they returned to their
original size and the right temperature, the incubation
would resume. It was better than the temperature-con-
trolled traveling case you had originally planned to use,
which would have been bulky and difficult to hide during
your travels.

You placed the glass eggs inside the incubator and left
the serpentarium as discreetly as you came. The corridor
to the hangar was empty. Arriving guests used Hyla's public
spaceport to dock their shuttles, then rode in carriages to
the palace. Only you, Elias, and the extended royal family
could use the palace's hangar, and your cousins had
already landed three days ago.

The *Starling* and its sleek design stood out next to the
transit shuttles you and Elias used to join the orbiting
Lifebringer. Its blue hue reminded you of Therria's sky that
you'd never see again, should you successfully remain in
hiding for the rest of your life. Even your cousins' ships
looked dull next to the racing ship.

You boarded the *Starling* and, after taking off the time-
suit and miniaturizing it again, sat in the pilot's seat, where
Marise used to sit. The ship's interface scanned you and

recognized you as an authorized copilot, which allowed you to ease the ship out of the hangar. Once the sky was above the *Starling*, and beyond, the vastness of space, you buckled your seat belt and readied yourself for the crushing acceleration. You hadn't flown for months—since Marise had become sick—but your body remembered how it felt, and before you pushed the throttle to lift off, adrenaline was already flowing through your veins.

II

Your story continues with change. After living as a princess your entire life, you were now about to become a different person. You had learned to be obedient and delicate and helpful and believed yourself unable to equal your brother because of that. What you were about to realize is that everybody can adapt who they are when facing adversity and change, yourself included. The woman I met had little to do with the princess she once was. Her travels across the galaxy changed her even before she became Green Scales.

The suits don't make the woman, but experience and time certainly do.

THERRIA'S SPACE TRAFFIC controllers didn't question you. The *Starling* belonged to a royal family and was exempt from regular procedures. As long as you traveled to a planet or station with Cician representatives, you would not be bothered. But only for a time. Once Elias realized you had disappeared, the search for the *Starling* would begin, and the farther away from the ship you were, the better.

A full day passed between your departure and the moment you made the crossing. You had passed the moon's orbit several hours ago, and you were drifting in the void between Therria and the closest planet, Rebos. The perfect location to open a wormhole without being spotted. You set the coordinates to the Vailar System and turned on the diastium engine apprehensively. Opening a wormhole had always scared you, despite the process being entirely managed by the ship's interface.

And there it was, before your eyes, in the darkness of space. It would remain open for a brief moment, enough for the *Starling* to make the crossing. You moved the ship closer to the eerie spherical structure, inhaled deeply, then plunged into the passage.

Only when the *Starling* emerged on the other side did you realize you'd be Elias's wife if you had stayed on Therria. Your heart sank as you imagined your companion panicking after finding your apartment empty. Elias, searching the palace from top to bottom, interrogating everyone and everything to discover where you were. Your mother, pretending to faint as the guards told her you had disappeared. *The princess is missing!* you imagined them shouting through the palace. *She must have been abducted!* They might believe it until Elias noticed the *Starling* was missing and the eggs in the incubator were fakes. Perhaps your mother would convince him that an intruder had abducted both you and Celadon's children, then forced you to pilot the *Starling*, but it didn't change the outcome. He would look for you. You had to disappear.

THE VAILAR SYSTEM was the most populated. An ideal place to hide among the crowd. Of the six planets orbiting its star, Vail, four were rich in diastium. The precious ore filled the ground of many planets in this corner of the galaxy, but it was most abundant on Phau, the second planet closest to the sun—and also your final destination.

You didn't set course for Phau. Instead, you flew to the edge of the Vailar System to dock and abandon the *Starling* in the Arnitha Station. It served as a travel hub between the Vailar System and its closest neighbor, a permanent, natural wormhole. The wormhole was connected to another system that was devoid of diastium but home to Xulia, a Therria-like planet. Its fertile soils fed Vailarian colonists, making diastium mining possible.

Arnitha had the biggest spaceport in the galaxy. Docks took up half the station and hotels, restaurants, bars, and repair shops occupied the rest. Royalty and rulers and ambassadors boarded and disembarked next to miners and merchants and farmers and anyone else brave enough to venture into this dark corner of space. No dedicated platforms. Everyone was treated equally on Arnitha when it came to the spaceport. Despite its eye-catching look, the *Starling* would go unnoticed among the hundreds of ships that docked there.

You gathered your belongings and food rations from the ship, put your hood on, and left the quietness of the *Starling* for the unrelenting crowd of Arnitha. In a clothing shop, you bought a new cloak—a light green one ideal for Phau's warm climate that would also match your snake-suit to perfection—and underclothing to wear under a suit.

Then you found your way to an hourly hotel where they didn't ask for your name when you booked a room.

The room was small and filled with stale air, making you wonder if the air filters actually worked. It compared poorly to the suites you were used to as a princess. It wasn't as terrible as it could be, for you knew the station harbored worse places, but to say it was clean would have been an obvious exaggeration.

First you took a shower, washing the tears and sweat from your body. Then you restored the snake-suit to its normal size and put it on. You acted absentmindedly, as on autopilot. There was no time to lament your fate. You placed the snake-mask on your face, carefully sticking it to your skin so it wouldn't fall unexpectedly. Finally, you collected your things and put the new cloak on, hiding your hair inside the hood.

If the hotel clerk found your attire bizarre, he didn't voice his opinion when you walked through the lobby and dropped the room key in the key drop box. Considering the eclectic clientele frequenting hourly hotels, he had probably seen worse. Your attire got you a few stares outside of the hotel, though. Not that people weren't used to colorful or dubious travelers—the station had its fair share of smugglers, pirates, and thieves crawling through its corridors—but a suit made of snake scales was, to say the least, unusual.

You waited in line for one hour to purchase a third-class ticket to Phau. You had the means to pay for better amenities, but at the cost of discretion. Not only would you need to show proper identification to purchase a first-class ticket, but no doubt other passengers would complain about you and your suspicious attire, bringing unwanted attention upon you. *Best to travel among people who won't complain about what someone looks like,* you aptly told yourself.

The ship taking you to Phau was named the *Rosebay,* which made you laugh bitterly considering how terrible it smelled on board. For ten days, you shared a cramped six-bunk cabin with twenty other people who left you alone only because of how terrifying you looked. One night—or rather, during *sleeptime,* since there is no day-night cycle in space—a passenger approached to steal the miniaturizer from your forearm, but you woke up immediately and told him you'd break his neck if he ever tried. You had spoken in your native Therrian-Cician, a language he didn't seem to understand, but he still froze. Perhaps it was because of the voice-warping device, or your murderous gaze, but he left without a word. You had never threatened anyone before, and you hadn't known you actually could. You obviously didn't have the strength to break anyone's neck, but to protect Celadon's children, you wouldn't hesitate to try. Of course, the passenger-turned-aspiring-thief didn't know about the eggs and only saw a fancy gadget he could resell for thousands of credits, but you weren't going to explain yourself. If you were to survive the journey, you had to exude toughness. Your attire helped, but you also had to play your part, and you surprised yourself at how well you were already playing it.

THE ROSEBAY LANDED in the biggest international city on Phau. Like most places on the planet, Darim City experienced stable weather all year due to Phau's small axial tilt. Here, it meant wet and hot all year, and you couldn't wait to leave as soon as you set foot outside of the shuttle. Your lungs weren't used to the humidity, and each breath felt like torture. You had already visited Phau, but only the Cician colony, located in a drier region. Of course, you couldn't go there, no matter how much your lungs begged you to. No; instead, you would seek refuge in the Ethilian colony, closer to the New Zankia region where Celadon's children belonged, yet far enough from your brother's clutches.

Ethil was a powerful country—an empire with colonies on every habitable planet known to humankind, and outposts on uninhabitable ones. Its relationship with Cicia ranged from mutual ignorance to outright rivalry, and that had included, two centuries ago, armed conflict on Xulia. Thankfully, the two countries had learned to tolerate each other and to compete for natural resources without resorting to war. Ethil's colony was an ideal place to hide, not only because you spoke the language but also because of its well-known unwillingness to accommodate Cicia's requests. Even if the emperor himself found you, he might decide to grant you asylum to infuriate Elias. You weren't ready to take your chances, though. No one could know Princess Cyrelle of Cicia was hiding among Ethilian colonists.

WHILE RIDING THE bus, your eyes were riveted on the wide screen above the sliding doors. It displayed itinerary information and brief headlines about local and interstellar news in different languages. The news of your disappearance should have reached Phau, you knew. Maybe the

Cician authorities had already found the *Starling* back in Arnitha. *Or maybe not*, you almost blurted when a headline reading "Search for the *Starling* and Princess Cyrelle continues on Therria" appeared on the screen. You kept staring at the screen a bit longer, expecting to see more details, but it switched to "Next stop: Bellevue." You exhaled slowly through the snake-mask. It was real. You were a runaway princess. Elias knew the *Starling* had a diastium engine, so it was only a matter of time before the Cician authorities searched other systems.

Every stop through Darim City made you flinch and glance at the doors apprehensively, as if you expected the city's police to board the bus and check everyone's identification. You had none. What if they took you to a police station and forced you to remove the mask? They could easily confirm your identity and bring you to the Cician border for Elias or one of his envoys to snatch you. That was, of course, only if Elias had issued an arrest warrant Darim City deemed justified; but while fleeing a wedding was no crime, stealing Celadon's eggs definitely qualified as such. Yet nothing happened, and soon the bus started its long drive through the rainforest.

The bus crossed the Ethilian border at dusk. You knew it only because an enthusiastic "WELCOME TO ETHIL" appeared on the screen. Border controls used to be strict and systematic, but decades of peaceful cohabitation on the planet and trade agreements had eased them. You were grateful for it, because you would have never survived a clandestine hike through the jungle.

When you reached the first city after the border, the driver's voice echoed in the bus, announcing this was the last stop. You followed other passengers outside, doing your best to ignore their sidelong glances. While space stations and international cities were full of odd people dressed worse than you, it would be different from now on.

It became an issue on the next day as you looked for a job. A princess born and raised, you had never worked a day in your life, but would work anywhere that would have you. The easiest would have been to offer your serening services to citizens, but it was too risky. Zephis's followers were rare on Phau, and Cyrelle of Cicia was a renowned Serenitress. With the news of your disappearance already made public, people would quickly make the connection. Instead, you tried hotels and restaurants and cleaning companies, but your appearance was so unpleasant that everyone bluntly sent you away. Not even the hotel you had stayed at for the night wanted you—neither for hiring nor for an extra night. So you packed your belongings and left for the next city.

You had no better luck there, nor in any of the other cities you visited as you kept journeying south. Soon you would have nowhere to go but back to Darim City, half your credits gone for nothing. The farther south you went, the better the climate became, but the closer to the Cician colony you were. There was a sea between the two colonies, but you still didn't like the idea of being so close. Living on the coast meant crossing paths with Cician merchants and envoys. No, that didn't please you at all, but you had no choice. The Ethilian colony was still the best place to hide on Phau while caring for the eggs and searching for the right place for them to hatch in the savanna. You wouldn't give up until every single potential employer had slammed their door in your scale-covered face.

After eight days traveling across the Ethilian colony, you resigned yourself to trying your luck in coastal cities.

Liphong and Calam seemed appealing because they had no spaceport and only small harbors that didn't see a lot of Cician ships, but that also meant fewer jobs and more close-minded people who wouldn't hesitate to drive you away unceremoniously. You crossed them off your list—at least for now—and boarded a bus for the only other Ethilian coastal city, which was also the third largest city in the colony. It was your last chance to find employment.

The bus had reached the top of a hill when the city's skyline loomed into view.

Prophis. A city like no other, one you had never seen with your own eyes and that you had never expected to seek refuge in. The city where you were about to meet me.

The majesty of the landscape did not escape you. Behind the city was the Auriverian Sea and its silvery waters dancing under a sun the clouds dared not hide too often. Prophis was far from the rainforest, and though its weather delighted tourists, the lack of rain made Prophisians nostalgic for the sound of water tapping on a window. We would pray relentlessly to the multifaced god Ystos for days, weeks, sometimes months during bad years, and when he finally answered our prayers for rain, all Prophis would celebrate.

But if Prophis craved rain, its lifeblood was of a different nature. The green dust that flowed through the city at nightfall reminded everyone that diastium made life possible here. There was only one mine in the entire Ethilian colony, and that mine was also the biggest on the planet, its production equaling that of the Cician colony and its five mines. Without Prophis's diastium, Ethil couldn't power the diastium engines of its fleet, which would condemn the empire to never-ending trips in cryogenic chambers instead of the instantaneity of crossing a wormhole. Diastium was time, and time was power.

You realized your best chance to find a job in Prophis was at the mine when, after getting off the bus, you found yourself face-to-face with a poster reading "Workers wanted all year round." Your first instinct was to look at the city map displayed next to the poster and locate the mining operation offices, and you considered walking there immediately, but your body disagreed. You had traveled for what felt like an eternity, taking little time to rest. Besides, Phau was a big planet with a gravity stronger than Therria's, and longer days. Visitors always needed time to adjust, and so did you. You could have used the moon-suit to relieve the pressure from your body by adjusting the gravity affecting you, but you couldn't wear it in public, for someone could recognize you. You had no choice but to spend the day in your snake-suit. The only times you had been able to use the moon-suit were the nights spent in the privacy of a hotel room, and there had been too few of them since landing on Phau. Your body needed one now.

The closest hotel was around the corner. Its name announced a comfortable and expensive place where you wouldn't go unnoticed—and where the clerk would likely tell you *Sorry, we're fully booked* when they were not—but you didn't have the strength to scout around for another place, so you were willing to spend extra credits to convince the hotel staff to let you in.

Fifty credits got you a "Let me double-check we really have nothing available," and your offer to bring that up to a hundred turned it into a long-awaited "You're in luck, I actually have something for you." You gritted your teeth and paid, adding an extra dozen credits to be allowed to reserve the lodging without showing identification or giving a name.

You cried when you entered the room. After sleeping in either cheap motels with bedbug-infested beds or overnight buses for over a week, the sight of a bathtub and clean bedsheets warmed your spirit as if you were serening yourself.

After soothing your body in a warm bath—one of those things that you took for granted when you lived as a princess, but were now a luxury—you put on the moon-suit and tweaked the gravity settings to feel lighter. Then you let yourself fall on the bed, closed your eyes, and slept a dreamless sleep.

FIFTHDAY 5 PRIMISUN 1496 AE
PROPHIS, ETHILIAN EMPIRE COLONY, PHAU

Knowing about how people live and travel outside of palaces is one thing, but seeing and living it is another. Nothing could have prepared me for these days. When I read my previous entries and the concerns I had about flowers in the gardens not being watered enough or my tailor-made dress being too tight, it all sounds superfluous. Some people live comfortable lives like the one I had in Hyla, while others live in conditions akin to that of the Rosebay every day of their lives and not only during a space transit.

My current situation isn't more enviable. My credits are running low. Soon I will have nothing left to fend for myself but my suits,

and I refuse to use them to commit crimes. (I
know I could easily steal food with the time-
suit, or trespass with the moon-suit.) I could
try selling them or their components, but they
are too precious to part with. No, I need to
work. Hopefully, the people operating the mine
will find a use for my skills. I may be meek and
dull, but I know how to use my hands and my
brain.

I pray to Zephis they see it.

"EVER WORKED IN a diaz' mine before?" the recruiter, a man with large shoulders and stubble on his chin, asked as you sat in front of him in his austere office. He had spoken in Phau-Ethilian, without the hint of a Therrian accent. A local, born and raised in the colony.

"No, I haven't," you answered matter-of-factly in Therrian-Ethilian, surprising him with your fluency. He must have expected you to answer something like *Sorry, I don't speak Ethilian* in Stellianto and been ready to switch to the interstellar speech.

"Well, there's always a first," he said. "As long as you know how to handle a pickaxe and a drill, you'll be fine. You've done physical labor before, right?"

You hadn't, and lying about something so easy to assess would lead you nowhere but outside the office, as jobless as you came. "There is always a first."

He frowned at you, as if expecting you to say you were joking. When he realized you were serious, he said, "Listen, I'm sure you've heard that we hire anybody and don't give a shit if they die on the job because there's always more bodies waiting in line outside. There's some truth to it, but I'm not dumb either. Working in the mine isn't for the faint of heart. If you can't do the job, the boss will kick you out, and he'll kick my ass for sending him good-for-nothings."

You gulped before saying, "I am certain I can still contribute to this operation."

His eyes opened wide, and he laughed. "What's with the fancy talking? You a professor or what? We need muscle here, not brains. You leave the brain to the boss and do as he says."

You silently cursed yourself for speaking as if you were welcoming an Ethilian delegation in Hyla's palace. "Don't you have any other jobs?"

He clicked his tongue and looked at you in silence. You could see on his face that he was hesitating between showing you the door and doing a good deed by helping a poor jobless woman. To your relief, he chose the latter and asked, "What have you done before?"

"I know how to pilot small ships."

"We don't need pilots here," he said, crushing your hopes. "Diaz' shipping is managed by another company, and they only take the best. If you don't have your license and all, they won't hire you." He paused. "What about machinery? Can you drive other stuff besides ships?"

"No," you whispered.

"That's it? No other experiences?"

"I worked as a temple assistant before." A half lie. You had never worked in a temple, but you knew enough about monastic life thanks to your mother and your serening training.

"Which one?"

"Not just one," you said, unwilling to pronounce Zephis's

name. "I would go wherever I was needed. Mostly minor deities' temples."

He looked at you from head to toe, visibly examining your attire, and said, "Well, it ain't what it used to be, their dress code, if they let you work dressed like a freak. You always wear that? Never show your face?"

"Yes," you said firmly, making clear it was nonnegotiable. "But I can wear protective equipment, of course."

He snorted. "Protective equipment? You'll be lucky if you get some. But you won't be working in the mine, missy. We've ruled that out already, right?"

"Right."

He let out a long sigh. "You ever cooked in these temples?"

"Yes, of course," you said. The palace had its own cooks, but a Cician princess's education included cooking and baking. "I learned from the best."

"The best, just that? Hey, we don't need you to cook up fancy meals. We've got hundreds of mouths to feed every day for lunch. It's all about being efficient."

You nodded. "I can cook large quantities."

"All right."

He handed you an application form. You filled it out as much as possible with mostly false but believable information, leaving all the optional fields blank. When came the moment to write your name, you paused. So far you had been able to avoid giving a name by sleeping in places cheap enough not to ask for it or by paying extra to request privacy.

"Don't remember your own name, hey?" he asked. "Or you don't want to share it?"

"It's complicated," you said, knowing it made a poor excuse, if even one at all.

"What happened? You offended a god and now you're hiding from his priests? That's why you're asking me to get you a job here instead of offering your services at the Temple of Purity?"

"I don't want to elaborate."

"Well, as long as you don't offend *our boss*, I don't really care about what you did or didn't do before walking into our office. But," he said, tapping the pen on the form where the empty name field was, "I still need a name here. Anything will do, as long as you answer to it."

You remained silent. Should you use your second or third name? No, it was still too risky. While most people only knew you as Cyrelle of Cicia, some knew your full name, Cyrelle Aimée Ludivia. You could go with Lude, perhaps? Or Divia? Both were different enough.

As you were about to say something, he lost patience, took the form, and wrote something down. Sliding it back to you, he said, "You're Green Scales, now. Like that awkward mask hiding your face. See? That wasn't hard. Now I just need a signature and you're in."

You stared at your new name on the form, too stunned by the man's choice to respond. Green Scales. That was how people saw you. A snake in human form. At least nobody would think of "Green Scales" as a runaway princess.

So you didn't argue, you signed, and Green Scales you became.

Your story is far from over. It is, actually, only beginning.

I don't know how you felt during your first day in the kitchen, for you were too exhausted after a hard day of work to pen your thoughts in your diary, so I can only draw conclusions based on what others told me. Anyway, you are used to me filling in the gaps by now, aren't you? I couldn't possibly know every single detail of what happened to you, what people exactly said, or what your expression was or what you thought when you spoke, not from a diary alone, even if you diligently wrote in yours almost every day. I do it so your story feels real to you. It needs to be vivid, like a true memory. It is important.

What I know for sure is that you are about to change into a different person. Your resilience is growing with every passing day as you meet people who will transform you for good. I pride myself on being one of these people.

Yes, my love, I am reaching the point of your story where we meet. But before I get to it, let me tell you about how you met the people of Prophis and slowly but surely became one of them, despite the challenges in your way. I wish they would have been easier on you, but my people have been hardened by a life of exploitation in the service of an empire they despise. As I recount the first months you spent among them, I hope you don't judge them too harshly, even if they deserved it at times.

THE KITCHEN SMELLED of fish and olive oil. Its supervisor, a short woman who asked you to call her Trizia, cursed at Aldo—the recruiter—after you refused to remove your mask.

She argued a bit more, but upon seeing that you wouldn't comply, ended up muttering, "I want you to wear a face mask over it when you're cooking. I also expect you to wear this"—she threw a white apron at you—"and to wash your hands, miss…"

"Green Scales."

"And a stupid name on top of that. I guess that's not what your parents named you."

Her nasty comment made you think about your mother. Holding back tears, you resisted the urge to snap back something meaner.

"Not that it doesn't suit you," she added, pursing her lips.

"Aldo actually picked it."

"You let someone else choose that nickname for you? Who does that?"

"I guess I do. I actually like it. As you said, it suits me well."

She snorted. "I suppose Aldo isn't that stupid after all. He remembered I only want Ethilian speakers in the kitchen—though I warn you, we speak *Phau*-Ethilian here, not that Therrian variant of yours, so you'd better get used to it. If there's a word you don't get, I'll explain it once, but not twice. Understood?"

An hour later, you were slicing onions and gutting fishes and peeling potatoes. Trizia had assigned you the least-desired stations in the kitchen, and though she didn't treat you worse than the others, she seemed amused by the constant teasing you suffered from them and did nothing to stop it. They mocked your looks and your speech, and while the idea of insulting them back tempted you a few times, starting a fight in the kitchen was the last thing you wanted. *I must keep a low profile,* you told yourself multiple times. *Just ignore them. Ignore them, and they will stop.*

They didn't stop. The only person who didn't partake in the teasing was a cook named Numa. He didn't speak to you directly besides basic demands, but the sympathetic looks he gave you each time he asked you to peel more potatoes soothed your spirit enough to keep you going.

When lunch time came, Trizia assigned you to a serving station. She was short on servers, she explained, and cooks had to fill in. You nodded and did as you were told.

The server working next to you didn't treat you better than the cooks had. "You're going to scare the miners," she said.

"Aren't they supposed to be tough?" you answered mockingly.

"Even tough people can feel disgust."

You didn't reply. As long as you kept your job, you couldn't care less about what people thought.

Shortly after the clock reached one thirty—Phau's

noon—the cafeteria became alive with miners and other workers walking through the door. They came from all the corners of the galaxy, their skins ranging from the palest white to the darkest shades. What they all had in common was the greenish dust covering their clothes and hair. Some even had diazdust—as they called diastium residue—on their face and hands. A handwashing station was available to them, but they didn't use it. Either they didn't have time, or they had given up on safeguarding their health. After all, eating a bit of diazdust would not make a difference if they had already inhaled it all day.

The teasing continued, from the miners this time. The polite ones would avoid eye contact with you as you put fried fish onto their plate, but the majority didn't hesitate to laugh and call you names. Only when a tall man who looked like he had never laughed in his entire life entered the cafeteria and shouted at everyone to keep moving did the miners stop bothering you. Everything about him screamed *I'm the boss*—the way he walked and talked, the half-scared, half-annoyed glances he received—and when a few miners muttered "Yes, sir," your intuition was confirmed.

Because I walked into the cafeteria after him, I didn't witness any of it and only know what happened because Numa told me. I did notice the sadness in your sapphire-blue eyes that only a fool would not want to drown in. Not only your eyes; the snake-suit and mask gave you an intriguing aura. Why did you wear that odd outfit under your apron? Your skin was so pale that I wondered if you wore the mask to protect it from the sun, but it looked too strange to be the only reason. Not only was it, like your suit, made of snake scales, but also scales of a unique green hue. The color of raw diastium.

Once everyone was served, Trizia gave you a break so you could eat. A strand of hair was sticking out of your hood, and you put it back inside nervously as you ate the potatoes you had worked so hard to peel. You didn't see me. I was a mere worker among others, and that's exactly what I wanted the boss and others to see. I didn't want anyone to notice me. But at that very moment, I wanted *you* to notice me so badly.

"That's Green Scales," a cafeteria employee picking up dirty dishes told me as he noticed my insistent look. "She started this morning. Wouldn't tell Aldo anything about her past. Not even her real name."

It only made me more curious. Who were you? What did you hide under that mask? I considered walking to your table and asking you, but something in your eyes—again, your eyes—convinced me you didn't want to answer. I also had other pressing priorities that didn't allow me to pursue mysterious strangers, no matter how alluring their eyes were. So I ate my lunch and left the cafeteria without looking back, ready to put our encounter behind me.

Your day wasn't over. In the afternoon, you cleaned the kitchen almost by yourself, Numa being the only one helping you. The other cooks didn't idle and busied themselves with preparations for the next day, but it didn't surprise you that they had left the most annoying tasks to you.

The sun was ready to set when Trizia finally told you to go home.

"Aldo said I would get a room in the housing building."

"Ah, of course," she said. "You're not from here. Should have guessed that with your Therrian accent."

Local workers who had their families in Prophis usually lived in the cheapest district of the city—the closest to the mine—but half of the miners came from abroad. For these men and women who came to Prophis without their families, the mine provided housing against a deduction from their salaries. The amount wasn't negligible, but it was still lower than renting an apartment in the city.

"I'm sure Aldo took care of it," she said. "Don't sleep in tomorrow. I want you at one hour past dawn. No later."

Before you could ask where the building was, she was gone.

"I'll show you," Numa said after seeing the confusion in your eyes.

He took you to the lobby of a three-story building, where its supervisor gave you a key labeled 306. It would be quieter on the third floor, Numa explained, but you would be far from the amenities on the first floor. You shrugged. You didn't mind walking up and down the stairs with laundry bags and trays of food. You had been used to servants handling chores for you, but you knew how to care for yourself and welcomed the isolation if that meant fewer people to bother you.

Before you went upstairs, Numa showed you the communal room where workers gathered to play Deji—a card game popular on Phau—and watch the news. You peeked at the screen, wondering if the search for your person had progressed, but all the journalists talked about was the ongoing investigation into a failed burglary attempt on the property of Prophis's governor. Authorities suspected the involvement of the Bronze Faction, an underground group fighting for independence that the emperor had declared illegal two Therrian years ago. You had never heard about them, but you had never heard much about non-Cician colonies—except for Elias's complaints about how a piece of land owned by another country should belong to Cicia.

"Too bad the Bronzees botched the job," a man seated in the assembly said.

"What do you think they were looking for?" another asked.

"Probably for your wife," a third said with a raucous laughter that the other miners echoed.

Numa clicked his tongue and whispered, "Don't mind them. They're not bad guys. Just people trying their best with what they have."

You didn't answer. These people had a hard job and poor working conditions, but half of them had insulted you a few hours ago. Some were already glancing at you again with mocking looks, as they were done teasing the other man.

"The mining company is owned by the empire," Numa said. "So technically, we're exploited by the emperor and his puppet—the boss. Diaz' is the most important resource in the galaxy, yet we're paid as if we were mining coal on Therria. You won't find a lot of empire sympathizers here."

That explained their reaction to the failed burglary—the governor represented the will of the emperor, after all— but not their rudeness. Still, you understood what Numa meant. They teased each other and whoever was an easy target because it was how they eased the pressure. Not an excuse, but an explanation. And if they had displayed cruelty toward you today, at least they hadn't asked for your dismissal. Not that you knew of. This place and its people were the first to accept you since you had left Therria.

You thanked Numa for his help and went to your room. It was small and equipped with the bare minimum, but it was yours. You didn't have to share it with another worker, which meant you could take off your attire and stop being Green Scales. Diligently, you checked that the key locked the door properly. Then you searched for a place to hide your belongings. Nobody had noticed the miniaturizer on your forearm since you had carefully hidden it under your suit, but you couldn't work with it every day. You were sure that if it got noticed, someone would try to take it—forcibly, perhaps—and all the threats in the galaxy wouldn't stop them. Regardless of its content, the miniaturizer itself was worth too many credits for an underpaid miner without principles to ignore. You didn't know yet who had principles and who didn't, but you weren't naive and assumed there was at least one would-be thief among them. Even I wouldn't have left my things unattended here, and they were the people I was fighting for.

Under the bed, you found a small cache. A former tenant had taken a slate off the floor and carved a space underneath. It wasn't as secure as the safes in Hyla's palace, but it was the best you had. Carefully, you put the miniaturizer and its precious contents in the cache before replacing the slate.

"I will find a proper home for Celadon's children," you whispered to yourself—and to Zephis and Celadon's spirit, too, in case they watched over you. "I will keep my promise."

A NEW ROUTINE quickly set in. Five days a week, you worked in the kitchen, doing whatever Trizia asked you to do. Your cooking skills were excellent, so eventually she assigned you to better cooking stations, and the rest of the team learned to interact with you politely—though I couldn't say that you had earned their respect yet. To them, you were still a quiet woman dressed in odd attire who refused to give her real name. Someone they couldn't trust.

On Sixthdays, the last day of Phau's shorter week, the mine stopped its operations for everyone to rest. All workers living in the housing building left for the day. Some attended ceremonies at the temple or strolled on the beach; most enjoyed themselves in the city's pubs. Numa invited you to join them for a lunch at their favorite local restaurant on the first Sixthday, then on the second, and stopped asking after you refused a third time. No one else ever asked you, and it suited you.

Instead, you spent every Sixthday in your room, wearing the time-suit to speed up time from your perspective and enjoy more of it by yourself. For each hour passing on Phau, you would experience two. Next to you, you wrapped Celadon's fragile eggs in the sun-suit to warm them gently so they could develop for a few hours under your watch. At first, you had considered combining the time-suit with the sun-suit to expedite the eggs' maturation, but what if something went wrong with the temperature, and you couldn't stop it before it was too late? No, it was best to be cautious. Zephis wouldn't forgive you if your carelessness caused the death of Celadon's children. You also didn't want them to hatch too soon, before you had a proper home for them.

Meanwhile, you read books about Phau's climate and geography that Numa kindly brought back from the library. When he asked why you were so interested in learning about the region but were unwilling to see it with your own eyes, you shrugged and said you preferred books to exhausting hikes. If he believed you, you couldn't tell, but the answer satisfied him enough for him not to ask again. The truth was that you were still scared of being caught despite your disguise. The more time you spent inside, the less likely you were to run into someone who could recognize you and bring you back to Elias.

What you were looking for, of course, was a place to take Celadon's eggs. It would have to be warm and dry—but not *too* dry—and rich in diastium and prey. You remembered the rocky plateaus from Celadon's memories and from Zephis's vision, and you hoped to find a similar place, if not *the* place—Celadon's lair. No one knew where it was exactly. Celadon had been captured outside it when she was still young, and the New Zankia region, where plateaus stood high around the savanna, spread over three different colonies. Zephis could have helped you, if she had wanted to. You prayed to her often, asking for a clue, but the goddess remained silent. Was she waiting for the eggs to be close to hatching to show you the path to Celadon's lair, or did she ignore you on purpose? Something in the back of your mind told you it was the latter. After what you had done, Zephis must have found it fitting to make you work hard for your salvation rather than deliver the answer on a silver platter.

In the late afternoon, before others came back, you went to the communal room to watch the news, on the lookout for information about your disappearance. More often than not, you left half disappointed, half relieved after seeing nothing about you, but sometimes the presenter said your name, and your heart raced.

One day you heard the *Starling* had finally been found, and the next Sixthday the presenter read a letter from Elias calling for all people in the Vailar System to share tips with the Cician authorities. He promised a reward to anyone who would help locate the place where you were held captive.

You let out a bitter laugh. As if you hadn't left of your own free will. Was it what Elias believed, or what he wanted people to think? He couldn't be so naive. He may have believed your mother's abduction story for a moment, but eventually he must have figured it out. He was too smart not to. No, he knew you had fled and wanted to save face. Pretending you had been taken would also convince hesitant people to help him find you. If they knew you had fled, perhaps they would be sympathetic to your cause and wouldn't come forward.

Such a liar and manipulator. Elias knew the cause of your sudden disappearance, yet he tried to make you someone else's victim when he was the sole culprit. It infuriated you so much that you squealed. You wanted to shout *Can't he leave me alone?* but you kept it to yourself. You were alone, but still cautious. Not cautious enough though, because your anger made you lose track of time, and you were still in the communal room when the others, myself included, started coming back. Quickly, you turned off the screen and stood up to leave. Everything would have gone well if Vark, one of the miners, hadn't been drunk and looking for trouble. You only knew his name and to avoid him, so it didn't surprise you when he rushed at you, his right hand ready to grab your snake-mask. You stepped back to evade him, but he seized your arm.

"Vark," I said, and he immediately froze. "Leave her alone."

He glanced at me, a gleam of haughtiness flashing in his eyes. I thought he would challenge me, but the glare I threw at him hit its mark, and he released you without a word.

The relieved look you gave me melted my heart, but I hadn't done it for you. Yes, you intrigued me, but the snake-mask covered half your face and prevented me from admiring your beauty. The more I think about it, I was already attracted to you, but I stopped Vark from assaulting you first and foremost because the Faction didn't need one of its members locked behind bars.

He walked toward me and muttered, "I don't trust that Green Scales, Sianna."

"You think I trust her?" I retorted.

"She was fumbling around in the communal room while we were all gone. Searching for clues. I tell you, she's a spy. Why would she hide her face otherwise?"

I frowned, considering his accusation. I suspected a spy to be among us—who wouldn't when leading a rebel group? —but you spent so little time among other employees that I doubted you could collect any valuable information to share with the emperor. As for Numa, he was careful not to tell you anything. You weren't interested in listening, anyway. All you cared about was doing your job and leaving as soon as possible to return to your room. So I said, "People have many reasons to conceal their identity in our city." I lowered my voice. "Numa watches her, too. If he sees her acting suspiciously, he'll tell me immediately. So far, she's only been reading books about Phau. The boring sort. She's a nature enthusiast, it seems."

"A nature enthusiast?" he said, too loudly for my liking.

I gritted my teeth. "Everyone is entitled to the hobby of their choice. Now, go back to your room before I decide to tell the boss how you harassed one of the cooks."

He grumbled, but did as he was told. I followed him until he reached his room and locked himself inside it. When I went back to the communal room, you were gone.

Why can't they all mind their own business?

I am tired of this life. There is no other way around it. Every day, I do my best in the kitchen, working as hard as everyone else, yet they can't stop teasing me like my stupid cousins used to do when we were children.

Children. No matter what Numa says, these people act like children.

It's all the snake-mask's fault. I am certain they would treat me very differently if they saw me in my sun-suit. They would see a princess radiant like Vail and would respect me. Instead, all they see is Green Scales. At best they fear me, at worst they mock me. I am glad this attire helps me hide my identity, but sometimes I wish I could be Cyrelle of Cicia in a glorious suit.

I understand it's difficult to trust someone whose face you cannot see, but why can't they be like Numa? Or like that woman, Sianna. She has never spoken to me, which means she has never insulted or mocked me either. People don't have to like me, but they can ignore me like Sianna does.

Does she really ignore me, though? She always glances at me when she picks up her lunch. At first, I thought it was mere curiosity, which I understand (I would be curious, too, if I met someone dressed like myself), but her glances are too frequent and too insistent. If it was not for today's events, I would have thought it was silent hostility, but she spared me a great deal of trouble by stopping Vark. I had to wait a long time for my heart to stop racing after he almost took off my mask in front of everyone, and my hands still shake a bit as I pen these words. If not for Sianna's timely intervention, my brother would probably already know where I am. She doesn't know it, but she protected me from a lot more than a fight with a drunk man.

I will have to thank her someday. Perhaps she could become a friend like Numa. She may be able to see beyond the snake-mask.

FOR MANY WEEKS, I kept thinking about Vark's words. Were you a spy? If you weren't a spy, then who were you? What were you hiding?

One Sixthday in the late morning, I was looking for Numa, since he hadn't shown up to our weekly meeting. This time, we had held it at the Underground Café—which, despite its name, wasn't underground at all and sat on the rooftop of a five-story building. After looking for him in his favorite spot in the city and not finding him, I assumed he had simply stayed home, either sick or too exhausted to join us. I wanted to check on him because no one else would. His wife had left him the year before, and, unable to afford his rent anymore, he had moved to the mine's housing building. He had no children, and his only brother had left Phau for Xulia ten years ago alongside their parents. Why he stayed in Prophis, working a job he hated, instead of joining his family on Xulia, I didn't know. I probed him a few times, telling him he didn't have to stay in the city if he wanted to reunite with his family, but he kept saying he cared too much about the Faction's cause to abandon us. After he added that he wasn't close to his parents and his brother, and considered us his actual family, I concluded that he genuinely loved Prophis and wouldn't leave until it was free from the emperor's grip.

Like yours, his room was on the third floor. I knocked on his door and called his name. After hearing no answer, I tried the handle. Locked. I put my eye to the keyhole, only to find the room was dark. Perhaps he was sleeping, but my intuition told me he wasn't there. I didn't force the door and resigned myself to leaving.

Except I didn't leave. I knew your room was nearby because Numa had told me, and I didn't fight the urge to walk to your door. Why did you spend so much time in your room? Was it because everyone mocked you outside of it? Numa had been kind to you. You could have made him a friend, an ally in a sea of foes. He could have introduced you to other people, convinced them to give you a chance, if only you had given *him* a chance.

Vark's suspicions echoed in the back of my mind. The emperor's efforts at disbanding the Faction had escalated, and after our recent failed attempt at recovering proof that the governor was misusing city taxes for his own benefit, the grip around us had tightened. No one had been arrested, but the governor's guards relentlessly raided places where they expected to find us. They had even interrupted a purification ritual at the Temple of Purity and ordered the High Priestess to let them search the temple's private quarters, despite her warnings that it would anger Ystos.

Were you a spy? I couldn't believe it—not with your attire. A spy must look trustworthy for others to confide in them, and you looked anything but that. But it didn't stop me from tiptoeing to your door and putting my ear to it. All I could hear was silence, but if you truly spent your time reading books, I wouldn't know it by eavesdropping. I'm not proud of it, but I put my eye to the keyhole, and it wasn't to check on your well-being—though I don't regret it. If I hadn't looked, I wouldn't have opened the door and met the real you under the snake-mask.

What I saw through the keyhole unsettled me. A figure sitting on a chair, moving faster than humanly possible, and an uncanny light that turned my blood cold instantly. Another person would have run away. I didn't. I still don't know what came over me, but I grabbed the handle and turned it. I pushed the door, but it didn't move. Locked. I could have left, but I tried again, putting more strength into my push, and this time the lock broke and the door swung open, revealing a scene forever etched in my memory.

Your first reaction was to drop your book and move toward your desk. You placed yourself between the wrapped eggs and me to hide them from my view. You moved so fast that I jumped. It worked, because I didn't see them, but the sun-suit still shone for an instant as you turned its light off, catching my attention. That was before I realized you weren't wearing your regular attire. Instead, you wore a suit as black as a starless night and nothing covered your face. I didn't know it was a time-suit, and I didn't understand what you did when you touched the controls to slow time back to normal, but after that, you moved at a regular speed again.

"Get out," you said with a feathery voice incomparable to the raspy voice that normally came through your snake-mask. If I hadn't noticed your eyes, I could have believed you were someone else and left, apologizing for the intrusion.

Instead of leaving, I squinted at you. I was seeing Green Scales's full face for the first time, and it was different from what I had imagined. What had I imagined? I don't know, but your nose and cheeks were more graceful than expected, and your lips were red like the sand covering Prophis's beaches. Your loose hair fell over your shoulders in delicate dark red waves, a rare color that mesmerized me. You looked eerily familiar, as if I had seen you before. But I was certain I had never met you. It was like seeing a celebrity in person after seeing their face hundreds of times on a screen. Except you didn't look like a movie star. The way you held your head, that slightly lifted chin, and that slightly trembling but commanding voice... You looked like someone used to being obeyed on command by servants attending your every need. You looked *royal*, and that thought immediately told me who you were.

"You're the Cician princess."

"You are mistaken," you said, but the gleam of fear in your eyes told me I was right.

I stifled a snort and slowly shook my head instead. I expected anything but for you to be Cyrelle, princess of Cicia, but it explained everything. Your shyness, the mask on your face, your sophisticated way of speaking Ethilian in an unmistakable Therrian accent. "By Ystos, Your Highness, I thought you were a spy of the emperor."

You frowned. "A spy?" You didn't correct me for addressing you properly, and you bit your lip when you realized it. You knew that I knew, and you couldn't do anything about it. No matter how I had managed to come in (Why did the lock break so easily? Had someone tampered with it?), not even your time-suit could take you back in time to prevent me from entering.

"Forget it," I said. "I was mistaken." You stared at me silently, not knowing what to say. I didn't know what to say either, so I introduced myself. "I'm Sianna."

After a few seconds that seemed like hours, you let out a sigh. You'd been recognized. Of course, you'd known it could happen, but you hadn't expected it to happen here, in the apparent privacy of your own room. To think, you had avoided leaving the premises to keep a low profile, and the real danger had always been here.

You cringed inwardly at how ironic the situation was—I had stopped Vark from revealing your identity in front of others, yet I had violated your privacy—and gestured toward me and said, "Close the door."

I carried out your request. Meanwhile, you watched me with an inquisitive gaze. My hair was a lot shorter than yours, barely reaching my shoulders. It reminded you of your mother's suggestion to cut yours. You loved long hair, not only on yourself but also on other women, yet you found my haircut to match my strong features to perfection. As for the reddish-brown tone of my skin, it reminded you of the ochre that is common on Phau and gives the planet its name in Stellianto.

But now wasn't the time to admire the face of the woman you still perceived as a threat, so you stopped staring at me and invited me to sit.

"This is probably not the place you expected to meet a princess," you said matter-of-factly.

I shrugged. "I didn't expect anything *royal* when I entered your room."

"What did you expect?"

"As I said, I thought you were a spy."

"What would I be spying on?"

I looked away. I couldn't tell you about the Faction. "Nothing that concerns you."

"Are you sure?" you asked, frowning. "What tells me *you* are not a spy sent by my brother?"

I smirked before saying, "I can guarantee you I'm not." As I pronounced these words, I realized you didn't look like a woman who had been abducted. "What are you doing in Prophis? All of Cicia is looking for you."

"Isn't it obvious?" you said sharply. "I am hiding from my brother. No one abducted me except my own conscience."

"So you didn't want that marriage," I said, feeling stupid for having considered you could have wanted it. The entire galaxy knew about the incestuous union you almost entered with Elias, and though it had shocked more than one person, it had looked like a consensual union. Only a small circle of people in the palace knew about your series of requests for impossible nuptial gifts, though others would have ascribed your wishes to a royal taste for excess if they had known. To me, the union had seemed like a terrible idea, but was still better than a forced marriage between a ruler and an unwilling commoner who was guilty of displeasing them. I should have known better than to assume your royal status would have protected you against a forced marriage. Nobody was equal to a king, not even his own sister.

"Of course I don't want to marry Elias," you said, glaring at me. "He is *my brother.*"

You said these last two words with so much disgust in your voice that I didn't contradict you. There was nothing to contradict, anyway. Brothers should not marry their sisters, kings and commoners alike, especially if the union is supposed to produce heirs. Cautionary tales about the Old People were full of dynasties ended because of diseases caused by inbreeding. But I still wondered if it was the only reason you had refused to marry him. "If he hadn't been your brother, would you have said yes?"

You lifted an eyebrow in surprise. "If you are asking if Elias is likeable or not, all you should know is that he is self-centered and only interested in making the kingdom—and himself—wealthier."

It answered only half of my question, but I couldn't blame you. I hadn't asked what I truly had in mind, and I wouldn't because it was an improper question to ask. I knew it because no one had ever asked me, even when the answer was plain as day.

"How old are you, Your Highness?"

The question surprised you again, and I saw you hesitate between telling me to stop interrogating you and wanting to pour your heart out. You hadn't spoken with anyone about your past life for months, and if you were honest with yourself, you craved a companion to share your feelings. But you didn't know me, so you simply said, "Twenty-six Therrian years."

"Twenty-six Therrian years and you found no acceptable suitor before your brother set his mind on marrying you."

"No," you whispered, "and believe me, my father—bless his spirit—tried until his last breath. But none of these men had what it took to make me happy."

I nodded, satisfied with the answer and unwilling to pry more. I had burst into your room and unveiled your biggest secret—two, perhaps, if I interpreted your latest statement accurately.

"There's a big reward for finding and handing you to your brother," I said matter-of-factly.

You clenched your fists and said, "Whatever he promises you, I will double it."

"I don't care about the money," I said reassuringly. It was mostly true. I only cared about freeing Prophis from the emperor's grip and making it an independent republic. Money could help reach such goals, but more than money, *you* could help me reach that goal. That meant doing something I was already ashamed to consider.

You see, the Faction was determined, but determination wasn't enough. Armed guards patrolled the governor's mansion day and night, and avoiding them was nearly impossible, as our failed burglary proved. The two Bronzees I sent that day only survived because they knew when to abort the mission to save their skins and live another day to fight the empire. And ousting the governor wouldn't mean the end of our worries. The emperor would send troops to regain control of the city.

People don't realize it, but a revolution is expensive, and not only in the lives sacrificed on the altar of freedom. For a coup to be successful, the Faction needed weapons, and to get weapons that rivaled those of the empire, it needed either money or allies. Since the Faction didn't have money, we had looked for allies. Powerful allies who despised the emperor as much as we did and who would be happy to protect us once we seized power.

Cician allies.

Despite the peace, Elias despised the emperor as much as the emperor despised him. And what could better secure the kingdom's support than returning the runaway princess to its king? If the promise to strike a favorable diastium trade agreement with Cicia and grant special privileges to Cician citizens in the city wasn't enough, *you* would be. And although I would feel guilty about delivering you to Elias, I would remind myself that you were one of them, after all. A royal who couldn't care less about commoners. You had fled Hyla's palace to save yourself when I had left my own to save others. That's what I thought, in that moment.

That I said I didn't care about the money made you unclench your fists, but you weren't duped. You were only half relieved and knew you weren't safe yet.

You looked me in the eye and asked, "What do you care about, Sianna?"

Your defiant tone surprised both of us. The past months had toughened you more than expected. As for myself, I didn't know what to think anymore. The Green Scales I had met hadn't impressed me with her physique or sharp tongue, but she still had a slightly threatening aura because of her attire. But once I knew she was a princess, I expected her to be a soft-spoken lady with little grit, because that's how women in the emperor's court were supposed to behave. I hadn't expected Cyrelle of Cicia to be… you. In a way, you were already more Green Scales than Cyrelle, even without your snake-attire.

"I care about a lot of things," I said. "The city. Its people."

You tilted your head. "You wouldn't be a Bronzee, would you?"

I tried to remain impassive, but the crooked grin that appeared on your lips told me I had let something show. You didn't give me time to react and quickly approached, grabbing my hand unexpectedly. I froze, but only for a second, because you immediately established a spirit-bond and delved into my mind without warning.

I shouted, or rather, I believed I did. My lips didn't move and the cry in my throat never went out, but you still heard it—in my own mind.

I had never been serened before, and thus had never experienced a spirit-bond. I didn't know what to do. My first reaction was to try pushing you out of my head, but I was too weak to repel a seasoned Serenitress. You could have easily seen my deepest secrets, though you only looked for what interested you and carefully avoided the most personal parts of my mind. The first thing you learned was my full name and my real identity. You felt my ever-present grief, though you didn't know who I had lost, and didn't seek to find out by intruding more. You saw how much I'd hated my life in an Ethilian palace, then the guilt I still felt every day about my mother and leaving her behind. The relief of reaching Prophis, not unlike your own feelings about your arrival in the coastal city. After that, you learned about my excitement to join the Bronze Faction, and the worries about leading a revolution and succeeding in making an alliance with a Cician emissary. This information told you enough about me, but not about my intentions, so you probed my immediate feelings. You couldn't find a sincere intent to turn you in, even if the idea had crossed my mind. You also saw my *other* conflicted feelings about you, but I wouldn't know it until later.

At last you broke the spirit-bond. I fell to my knees, holding my head between my hands. "What have you done?" I whispered, a tremor in my voice. I wanted to vomit.

Establishing a spirit-bond without the other person's consent was contrary to the rules you had learned at the Temple of Serenity, but you were merely defending yourself. Surely Zephis would understand. If you were captured, you couldn't keep your promise to the goddess to care for Celadon's children.

Still feeling a pang of guilt for causing me pain, you

asked, "You have never experienced a spirit-bond before?"

"No," I answered after a moment, which made you bite your lip. The first spirit-bond was always difficult, but an unwanted one was worse, especially without serening in the end.

"Then," you said, helping me to stand up, "please accept my apology, Lady Avasia—"

"It's Sianna," I snapped as I got on my feet. You had learned my full name, Avasiannata, but I would not let you pronounce it, especially not with a *lady* before it. You would call me Sianna like everyone else in Prophis did.

You nodded, understanding, and helped me sit on the bed.

"Why did you do this?" I asked, my eyes closed as I tried to soothe the pain in my head.

"Because," you said with a light snort, "you made an implicit threat to deliver me to my brother. If you don't care about the reward, I had to know what you had to gain. I had to understand how much of a threat you are."

I exhaled. "And what's your verdict?"

"You're a fool."

I clicked my tongue but didn't argue. I wanted to ask you why, but the pain made it hard to think or speak. Was it because you disagreed with my ideas? Or had you seen a flaw in the negotiations I was conducting with the Cician emissary?

"I can ease the pain," you offered, in lieu of an explanation about why you deemed me foolish.

"By doing another spirit-bond? No, thank you."

You raised an eyebrow. You had offered me a free serening ritual, not expecting the customary honorarium Serenitors received for their services, and I had bluntly refused. But after what you did to me, you understood, so you didn't insist. "I have medicine, if you prefer that."

"Painkillers?" You nodded. "How do I know you won't try to poison me instead?"

You sighed. "You have my word."

I wish it had been enough, but it wasn't. Not yet. So I shook my head and said, "I'm already feeling better." A lie, but I couldn't bring myself to let you enter my mind again or to accept a medicine I didn't trust.

"Very well." A pause, then you said, "I didn't know you used to live in a palace, too. Are you related to the emperor?"

"I'm his stepdaughter," I said bitterly. "I'm not his heiress and have no interest in being such."

"Why did you flee the palace?"

"The emperor forced my mother and me to join his so-called family."

You sat next to me. "I sensed guilt about your mother, as if you were responsible for her situation."

"It's a long story," I said, exhaling. "But to make it short, my... rebellious behavior didn't go unnoticed and led the emperor to force my mother to marry him when she couldn't tame my democratic ambitions."

You gave me another of your inquisitive looks, encouraging me to continue. Only a few people in Prophis knew about my past, and I would have never told you so early on my own. Yet you had seen fragments of my memories, and it had hurt like a thousand needles in my brain, but I didn't blame you for forcing the spirit-bond on me. I should have been upset at you, but I wasn't. Maybe it was because I had imposed my presence on you, unveiling your own secrets. None of that would have happened if I hadn't let my suspicions—or, more honestly, my curiosity—overtake me. It was I who entered your room without permission, forcing you to defend yourself with the only weapon you had. I could only blame myself.

There was also something in your eyes that made me want to tell you more. I believe what I saw was *understanding*. Compassion, perhaps.

So I continued, doing my best to ignore the persistent headache. "I was only fourteen when I started gathering other teenagers to fill their heads with what the emperor called 'anti-state propaganda.' My father was a low-rank noble, the last child of his parents. He wasn't a republican at heart, but he had himself married a merchant's daughter, refusing to obey his parents, who wanted him to marry a noblewoman. He encouraged me to read about philosophy and politics. He had books about the Great Republics of the Old People, philosophical and political treatises. I learned about elections, representatives, checks and balances, and how they improve the lives of the people. Things that don't exist in the empire and in your kingdom either, I guess."

You nodded silently.

I looked at you, trying to get a sense of your opinion, but you looked unmoved. "I don't expect a princess to agree, or even to understand."

You remained quiet. As a princess, you had received the best possible education and knew exactly what I was talking about, but you had also learned to accept kingdoms and empires and not to question your own position. Even your mother, an orphan raised in a temple, never questioned the monarchy she willingly became a part of. You had followed the path you were born into, neither agreeing nor disagreeing with it. It simply *was*. But your perspective had naturally changed when your brother tried forcing you to marry him. For the first time in your life, you had become the victim of an autocrat and realized the chaos a single man can cause when no one can stop him.

It would have been easy to blame the man and not the monarchy, to call him a mad king and pray for a better sovereign who cared about his people, and for a time, you did. But your certitudes had been shattered in Prophis when you witnessed firsthand how the emperor wasn't more popular among Ethilian commoners than Elias was among your people.

"When I became enough of a troublemaker to catch the emperor's attention," I continued, "my father was already ill and unable to keep me under control—and my mother was too busy caring for him to worry about a rebellious teenager. His death didn't calm me down—quite the contrary."

"So he is the one you grieve," you said softly. "I lost my father, too. I miss him every day."

I nodded. "I miss mine too. Not only because he was a good man, but because his death allowed the emperor to enact his plan. Instead of putting me in jail and making a martyr out of me, he had a cleverer idea. He made my mother his third wife and moved us to his winter palace on Phau, so he could keep a close watch on me."

You frowned. "So Ethilian men can still have multiple wives? I thought this custom of yours had fallen out of fashion and even been outlawed by the previous emperor."

"It has, but our current emperor doesn't burden himself with following the rules," I said bitterly. "He keeps it a secret, even if not guarded as well as he wishes."

"I wouldn't be surprised if my brother knew and if it gave him ideas . . ." you muttered. If the emperor disobeyed Ethilian law to marry more than one woman, Elias could disobey Cicia's to marry his sister. The only difference was your brother's willingness to do it publicly, when the emperor tried to hide his own transgressions. You didn't know which was worse.

"No one sees the second and third wives," I continued. "Only the first wife lives in the Ethilian capital on Therria alongside the emperor, and only her children can ascend to the throne. The other wives enjoy a comfortable life, but live in the shadows in colonies. For those who choose it, it can be a pleasant existence, but neither my mother nor I had desired it."

I paused and rubbed my temple. You moved your hand, silently offering to serene me again. Instinctively, I caught your hand to stop you, not realizing that one touch was all you needed to delve into my mind. But you didn't do it.

"I can do a minor invocation," you offered. "No spirit-bond. No medicine. If Zephis answers it, you will feel better."

"Does it really work?" I muttered. "Do the gods answer?"

"If you have faith in them, it does," you said, only half convinced by your own words, considering how Zephis had ignored you for months. You hid your uncertainty well enough so I didn't notice. Hopefully, you thought, the goddess would answer this call, since it had nothing to do with Celadon.

I considered your implied question in silence. Did I have faith in the gods? I had never been overtly pious. I prayed to Ystos because everyone else did in Prophis—and he was a god better to be in good graces with, should you need his help to grow your crops or to challenge another god's unjust decision—but that was it. My maternal grandfather used to ask Fortuners for Eterion's blessing, believing it would help his commerce to flourish, and maybe it did. Later, my mother taught me prayers, but I had never felt that intimate connection with Eterion or any other god people like you experienced. Still, I had nothing to lose, so at last I nodded and said, "Let's try it then."

You cleared your throat. "I will need my hand for that."

I blinked, then realized my hand was still squeezing yours. I whispered an apology and released it. After asking if you could touch me, you placed your palms on my forehead and whispered a brief prayer to Zephis.

As soon as the prayer ended, a gentle warmth filled my head, chasing the pain away. A blend of relief and bitter disappointment briefly seized your heart as Zephis answered the invocation, proving you right. The goddess willingly ignored your pleas for help to achieve the mission she had given you, but had no trouble answering your calls for other matters. At least, you told yourself, you could soothe me, and it was all that mattered in that instant.

Did I feel better because Zephis answered your invocation, or was it feeling your touch on my face? A bit of both, perhaps.

I smiled and said, "Thank you for the invocation."

"My pleasure," you answered, and I swear you blushed a little, but your face hardened and you quickly changed the topic, going back to my life in the emperor's palace. "So your mother was forced to become the emperor's third wife as a punishment for being unable to control you, yet you were considering condemning me to the same fate?" You paused, waiting for a reaction, but I didn't answer. "What is my crime, Sianna? What did I do to deserve this?"

"Nothing," I said, and sighed. "You did nothing. I... saw an opportunity. How could I not see it? I hadn't decided to actually do it. I was merely exploring the idea. You saw it when you delved into my mind, didn't you? That I didn't truly mean it."

You nodded, but you still asked, "Are you done exploring it?"

I lowered my gaze. "Yes. I won't condemn you to the same

fate as my mother." I already had a hard time forgiving myself for what had happened to her. I'd never forgive myself if I did the same to you. "Also, you said I'm a fool. I suppose that's because giving you to Cicia won't get me the support I need?"

You nodded and explained, "Cicia will give you everything you ask for, but they will give you *more*, and you will regret it bitterly. Only fools trust my brother not to do more than what he promises."

"What do you mean?"

You folded your arms and legs and sighed loudly before saying, "First, tell me why you came to Prophis and how you founded the Bronze Faction."

Fine, I thought. It was only fair to share more about myself before you'd agree to help me. "I didn't create the Faction," I explained. "It had already been active for years when I arrived in Prophis. I talked to the right people, and the Faction's recruiter eventually contacted me. After a few more meetings, he introduced me to the actual founder of the Bronzees. Once he learned I was—" I gulped. "Once he learned I was *Lady Avasiannata*, I was immediately invited to join their ranks. My reputation preceded me, so they were happy to have a personal enemy of the emperor. It didn't take long before I became an important member."

"But wouldn't the emperor find you and bring you back to his winter palace if he knew you were in the Faction?"

I snorted. "Well, he doesn't, and only a couple of Bronzees know my identity. There's no official search for me like there is for you. It would probably be too much of an embarrassment for the emperor to admit publicly that I had slipped through his fingers. But I know there are spies aware of my escape who would be delighted to find me. So I keep my past and my name to myself and share it only with people I trust. Besides the founder, Numa knows." You had seen him in my mind, so there was no point in hiding that he was a Bronzee too. "That's it. To the rest, I'm only a dedicated woman serving the cause."

"You do more than serving," you said. "I saw it, Sianna. You lead these people."

"I'm one of the two leaders, yes. The founder eventually offered for me to be his equal. We always proceed to a vote when we make important decisions, and my vote and my coleader's aren't more important than that of a regular member, but he still didn't like being the only person leading the group. He thought having another leader alongside him would bring more balance."

You nodded quietly, then asked, "So, why Prophis?"

I didn't need to think twice before answering. "Because it's the most important place in the empire. Without Prophis, the empire is nothing, and without the empire, Prophis could be *everything*. If there's one city on Phau that could be a true democracy, that could be independent and successful, this is it. We have a diastium mine and a port to trade diaz' with other nations. We have a ruthless sun that grows our crops and a powerful god who blesses us with rain when we need it. And most importantly, we have people who are tired of being exploited and who are willing to take their fate in their own hands. That's why I chose Prophis.

"If I could convince all the gods to help me, I'd make the entire colony an independent nation led by its citizens. But I know from my readings about the Old People's Great Republics that it's best to start small and let the republican ideal spread like wildfire. When other cities see how successful and happy Prophisians are, they'll want the same for themselves, and we'll gladly help them. Prophis first, the entire colony next."

To my surprise, you let out a soft whistle that could have been genuine admiration or gentle teasing. "I see why the Faction's founder offered you to become his equal," you said at last. "You are an eloquent woman, Sianna."

I didn't answer and gave you a faint smile.

"You are eloquent, and you care about Prophisians as much as the emperor should care about them," you continued. "I saw it. You aren't a mere idealist. You have a plan."

"Yes," I said. "We have already gathered enough popular support. Most Prophisians are already convinced of the emperor and governor's lack of interest in them, and even if we failed to collect the documents that'd prove their corruption, their acts already speak for themselves. If we were to stage a coup, people would gather in the street to cheer. They would walk to the governor's mansion and oust him themselves. But only if we can force the guards to surrender and not shoot at the crowd. For our revolution to be as bloodless as possible, we need Cicia's support. I can't go in with my men to arrest the governor without weapons. We'd be captured at best, executed on sight more likely."

You nodded, but then you said, "Do you really believe my brother would allow Prophis to become an independent republic?"

Your tone told me it was a rhetorical question and the answer was no, but I still shared what had been my reasoning until today. "If he can strike a profitable arrangement with us, why not?"

"Because Elias always wants *more*. Prophis has the biggest diastium mine on the planet. Don't you think he would want it for himself?"

"He already owns five other mines," I naively argued,

"and sells most of their production to foreign countries."

What you knew, and that I didn't, was that not only was Elias greedy, but he had also lost Celadon and her eggs. He couldn't afford to sell his diastium production anymore, and already the shipments to other countries had decreased. To regain his fortune, Elias needed to find you and the eggs or seize Prophis's mine.

You didn't tell me, and instead you said, "Trust me, he will betray you as soon as he sees the opportunity. He will let you throw the governor in jail, only to invade Prophis to supposedly 'restore order.' The emperor will want to intervene, of course, and it could escalate into a conflict between Cicia and Ethil—"

"Your brother wouldn't be so stupid as to start a war with Ethil," I said, unconvinced.

"You underestimate his greed, Sianna. But no, there would probably be no war. There would be lengthy talks and negotiations. Elias wouldn't claim Prophis and would pretend to be there only temporarily until Ethil could properly restore its authority. But he would treat it as his nonetheless, mining and shipping as much diastium as he could to the Cician colony across the sea. And if he is *really* good, he could convince Prophisians that it's in their best interest to join Cicia, and stage a pseudo-popular vote—"

"Prophisians would never choose to join Cicia. They won't submit to another autocrat."

"I believe you, but Prophisians can be *convinced* by other means than words."

"Fear," I muttered.

"Exactly. And this could still lead to war, of course. Regardless of what Elias does once Cicia moves to take Prophis, I can only foresee a negative outcome for the city."

I considered asking how you could be so sure Elias

would do it, but I didn't. You knew your brother. You had seen his political schemes.

"But we need these weapons to arrest the governor," I finally said.

"I understand, but you shouldn't get them from Cicia."

I gritted my teeth. "No one else wants to support us. It's either Cicia, or hiring mercenaries and buying weapons we can't afford."

"The weapons could be tampered with, Sianna," you said softly. "Elias already did it once."

I stared at you in disbelief. You gave me a rueful smile and explained what your brother had done. "Two Therrian years ago, Cician informants learned that a group of rebels had planned an attack against Elias on Xulia. Like you, they needed weapons. One of Elias's spies posed as an arms trafficker willing to sell them weapons for a low price, pretending to sympathize with their cause. Only, the weapons he sold them could be detonated remotely. On the day of their planned attack, Elias himself pressed the button as he stepped out of his ship, and the rebels never got a chance to approach him. I saw him, Sianna. I was on the ship with Elias. He laughed as he told me about his 'brilliant little plan.' I didn't feel bad for the people who had tried to take his life. Elias had simply prevented an assassination attempt against him. Who wouldn't? But the method he used shocked me. It was so cunning, so deceitful."

I shook my head. I had never heard about it. It had never been in the news. Newscasts in every country would have talked about how the king had escaped a murder attempt thanks to the kingdom's intelligence if Elias had made it public. No, he had kept this information confidential so he could use the same plan against others—against the Faction.

You put your hand on my arm, making me tense in surprise, and said, "Elias may have ordered the emissary to give you similar weapons so he can eliminate the Faction when he doesn't need you anymore."

I hadn't believed your brother to be better than the emperor, but now I knew I would never ally myself with Cicia. Not if Elias was its king. "What should we do, then?" I asked. "I'm supposed to meet again with the emissary tomorrow." I couldn't believe I was asking you for advice. We had just met, yet I was ready to trust you. Could it be the spirit-bond? Sometimes, when two minds merged, the persons felt connected afterward, as if they had known each other forever. My own mother had undergone a serening ritual once in the winter palace to appease her distress and had felt close to the Serenitress performing the ritual afterwards, as if the priestess were a long-lost childhood friend.

But if the spirit-bond had made me more inclined to trust you, I knew it was something else, too. We had a lot in common, and you knew Elias's mind. After everything you had shared with me, I couldn't help but feel like an idiot. You were right. I had been a fool to believe a kingdom would support an aspiring democracy. We would have been mere pawns in the game between Ethil and Cicia.

You didn't answer my question immediately and looked down, thinking. Eventually, you said, "Go to the meeting and keep discussing as if you are still planning to make an alliance with Cicia. Don't give the emissary any reason to believe you are walking out. Then, without warning, without Cicia's help, take control of Prophis."

"How?" I asked, confused. "And what about Cicia still invading the city? And the emperor? Even if we manage to take the city without Cicia's weapons, we won't hold it for long if we're defenseless."

"Cicia won't be prepared. It will take them weeks to assemble troops ready to take the city. Same for the emperor. Once you have Prophis, you have control of the mine. You can buy all the help you want with it. You have leverage."

It was true, but I still didn't see how we could oust the governor. "That doesn't solve the first problem. Taking control of the city in the first place."

"What if I told you I have the means for the Faction to depose the governor without bloodshed and without weapons?"

When I didn't respond, you gave me a broad smile and said, "What I am wearing now is a time-suit."

You explained its effects, and how I could use it to speed up time to the point I would become so fast, no guards could stop me before I had disarmed them. You even demonstrated it to me, and I watched with wide eyes when you moved three times faster than normal, grabbing the purse attached to my belt before I could react.

"That's not all," you added. "I have other suits. Would you mind leaving the room for a moment, so I can change?"

I nodded and left the room, still amazed by the time-suit. As I waited behind the door, you removed the eggs from the sun-suit and miniaturized them. You had agreed to share your wonderful suits with me, but Celadon's eggs were off-limits. If things went awry during the Faction's coup and we ended up captured, you didn't want me to know. What if I betrayed you and told the governor? He would either want the eggs for himself or would trade them with Cicia. No, I couldn't know. After hiding the miniaturized eggs, you put the sun-suit on and restored the moon-suit to its normal size, and then you called me back inside.

My jaw dropped when I saw you wearing the sun-suit, and I whispered, "So that was the eerie light I saw through the keyhole."

You told me how the sun-suit could emit light and warmth. Because using the sun-suit at its full capacity would harm its user, it wasn't the most powerful suit, but it could still be useful. Then you showed me the moon-suit and explained how its gravity-control technology could allow its wearer to sneak easily into the mansion to open the gates for other Bronzees. Meanwhile, more ideas popped into my mind about the suits' potential. Not only could you manipulate time, light, and gravity, but the suits were also made of diaston, the sturdiest fiber in the galaxy. Whoever wore them would be well protected against bullets.

"Are these secret technologies used by the Cician army?" I asked, unable to imagine another explanation.

You lowered your gaze and sighed. "No. These are the only suits. They were supposed to be nuptial gifts."

"Nuptial gifts? For your marriage with Elias?"

You nodded, and after a moment of hesitation, you told me everything—or almost. Marise's death and your brother's proposal. Your mother's idea to ask for impossible nuptial gifts, and how Elias delivered every single one of them. Your last request—Celadon's death—and how you lied about having a vision from Zephis. Guilt filled your voice, and though I wasn't pious, I knew how bad your lie was in the eyes of your goddess. You didn't mention Celadon's eggs—though I wish you had told me then, for it would have spared us much of the trouble we encountered later, since I could have helped you hide them—and only spoke of your real vision from Zephis, pretending the goddess took pity on you and showed you how to escape instead of ordering you to take the eggs to Phau. A small lie that would have big consequences later, but I can't blame you for not telling me then. You were still learning to trust me.

I listened silently, lapping up your every word with confusion and anguish. You told me how you got the snake-suit and the snake-mask, how you fled to the Vailar System, and how you stopped on Arnitha Station for a few hours before boarding a shuttle to Darim City. Eventually, you reached the moment Aldo agreed to hire you to work in the kitchen, then you fell silent.

I didn't know what to say, so I remained silent, too.

At last you said, "Do you often think about your mother?"

The question surprised me. After a moment, I nodded slowly and said, "More often than I'm willing to admit it. She's still in the winter palace, but I know she's doing well. Not *well*," I added after a pause, "but well enough. I send her terse, anonymous messages when I can so she knows I'm fine, too. What about *your* mother?"

You hadn't considered sending an anonymous message to her. You worried it would be intercepted, which would still be dangerous even if you used coded language only she could understand. Was she well, you wondered? Elias must have interrogated her, but he wouldn't harm her. She was still his mother, and no deity would forgive a son for hurting his parents. Filial love wouldn't stop him, but he wouldn't risk angering Eterion when fortune had escaped him.

"I don't know how she is doing," you whispered with a heavy heart.

"I could leverage my network and get someone on Therria to visit her temple. Just to confirm she's well, if sending a message is too risky."

A gleam of gratitude flashed through your eyes. "You would do that?"

"Yes," I said, nodding. "It isn't much."

You wanted to hug me, but you restrained yourself and only said, "Thank you, Sianna."

After another silence, I asked, "Why do you want to help me?" Was that the spirit-bond, too? Surely, as a Serenitress, you would know to ignore the effect. Unless it was too strong this time. You had seen more in me than you usually saw when serening people. "Why are you willing to risk so much for a city you don't care about?"

You opened your mouth to answer, but closed it after a second. You had almost said that since I knew about your identity, you had no other choice but to offer me an alternative to delivering you to Elias. But it wasn't true. You had believed me when I said I wouldn't do it. Also, you had seen my nascent feelings for you during the short but intense spirit-bond we had shared, and they had troubled you. In truth, you wanted to help *me* more than you wanted to help the city, and if the city mattered to me, then it mattered to you. Perhaps it was because of the spirit-bond, you considered, and the thought would fade in a few days. Or perhaps it wasn't, and it wouldn't.

Either way, you weren't ready to acknowledge your own complicated feelings for me, so instead, you gave me a practical, reasonable answer. "I won't pretend to care about the city as much as you do, but it is my home now. The only place that welcomed Green Scales. Also, if I don't help you and you fail, Prophis may fall under Cicia's control, and I would have to flee once again. I am tired of running, Sianna." If you had been fully honest, you would have also mentioned how protecting Prophis from Elias meant protecting the eggs from him, but again, you didn't trust me with this information yet—and everything you had said remained true. You didn't want to flee again. Once had been enough trouble for the rest of your life.

I nodded as a blend of excitement and apprehension filled my chest. "So, we're doing it," I said, extending my hand. "We'll take Prophis together with the Faction and your suits."

You took my hand and shook it carefully, saying, "We are doing it. We will free Prophis."

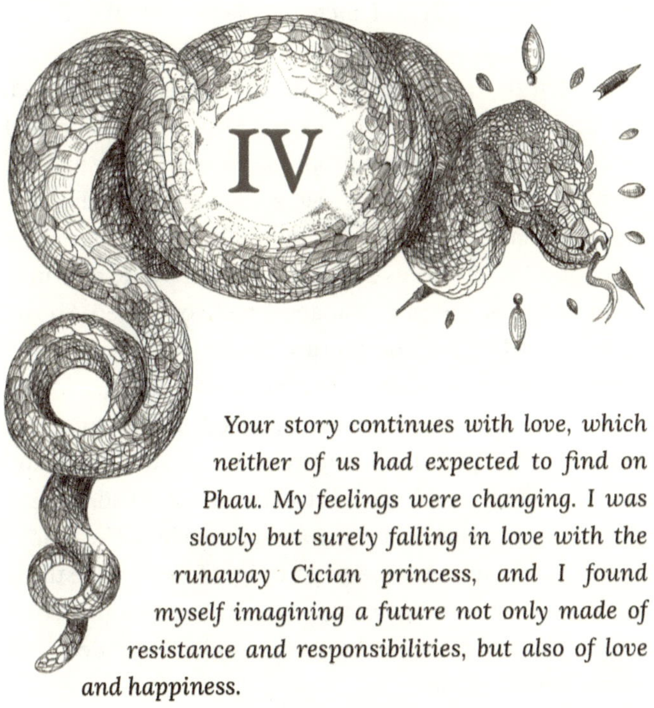

Your story continues with love, which neither of us had expected to find on Phau. My feelings were changing. I was slowly but surely falling in love with the runaway Cician princess, and I found myself imagining a future not only made of resistance and responsibilities, but also of love and happiness.

I didn't know if you would ever return my nascent feelings, and a part of me found it premature to harbor such considerations when my duties dictated that I care for the city first, myself second. I had to focus on my goals. Yet, I found myself thanking your goddess for putting you in my path by sending you to Phau, for your presence was a blessing to both my heart and Prophis.

It is a cruel irony that the same goddess eventually took you away from me.

AS YOU SUGGESTED, I met and dealt with the Cician emissary as if I still needed the kingdom's support. I pretended to be unsatisfied with the terms he proposed, but promised that I would discuss with the Faction and come back with another proposal. It was only a half lie; even if I had no intent to strike an agreement with Cicia, being a leader didn't mean I could make major decisions without other Bronzees' support. I would have to convince them to follow the plan you and I had concocted. So the emissary and I agreed on a future date to pursue our negotiations, and he left untroubled and unsuspecting.

The next Sixthday morning, I knocked at your door. You were already up and wearing your snake-suit, expecting me. Your green cloak hid your hair and forehead, leaving only your eyes visible above your snake-mask. The miniaturizer was tightened around your right forearm, the three suits inside the storage compartment. The two miniaturized eggs lay safely in the cache under your bed, still unbeknownst to me.

You followed me quietly through the streets of Prophis, unaware of our destination. Unlike last time, the Faction wasn't meeting at the Underground Café. We met at a different time in rotating locations every week, and I informed members of the chosen place only an hour in advance. This week, I had picked an actual underground location, the storage room of Verio's Books, a bookstore selling both paper-books and chip-books for reader-screens. Its owner wasn't a Bronzee himself—too dangerous for his liking—but sympathized enough with the cause to let us use his store. The high taxes he had to pay, which never seemed to be reinvested in Prophis's development, had convinced Verio more than any of my speeches.

I walked ahead of you into the bookstore, where Verio

busied himself stacking shelves while waiting for the first customers.

"She's with me," I said as you joined me inside.

He glanced at you inquisitively, and you said, "My name is Green Scales."

"That's quite fitting," he said after a brief silence. Then he turned and resumed stacking books as if he were alone.

You followed me to the back, where we found the staircase leading to the storage room. Downstairs, a diastium lamp sitting on a table cast a greenish light onto the shelving units covering the walls. The diastium lamp had been in Verio's family for three generations, left over from a time when oil lamps—too dangerous around so many paper-books—were the only alternative in an off-the-grid, newly established settlement. It had been using the same old piece of low-quality diastium for the last fifty Therrian years. A waste of diastium, some would think, since the ore had more value when refined to power diastium engines or to make diaston. We could have flipped the switch to use the lightbulb hanging from the ceiling instead of using such a rudimentary technology, but Verio always took out his old diastium lamp when we visited, as if the illegal nature of our meetings required us to meet in semidarkness.

We waited quietly for other Bronzees to join us. They arrived one by one, and soon a dozen people sat on the floor around us. Numa first frowned when he saw you next to me, but quickly a large smile spread across his face. As for Vark, who didn't expect to see you any more than you expected to see him, he stared at you incredulously before giving me a questioning look tinged with a hint of disapproval.

Next to me stood Jovien, the founder and other leader of

the Faction. He was old enough to be my father, and of a complexion darker than mine—not only because of his parentage but also because he spent countless hours under Phau's sun, praying to Ystos for rain. With his long indigo robe, his shaved head, and the three-face brooch pinned to his chest, you immediately recognized him as a Cleanser—a follower of Ystos trained in the art of purification—who had taken priesthood. As far as you knew, Ystos's priests had to stay outside of politics, but the confidence he exuded persuaded you not to ask him how he reconciled his vows with his political commitment. It could have been that Ystos himself had tasked the man to cleanse Prophis of the empire's corruption.

I introduced you as Green Scales, keeping your true identity to myself as we had agreed. Vark didn't like that and didn't refrain from telling others.

"I know who Green Scales is," I said, "and she has valid reasons not to let anyone other than myself know at the moment."

"Not even Jovien?" Vark argued.

"Not even Jovien," I said.

Jovien nodded and said, surprising you with the depth of his voice, "I trust Sianna's judgment. She briefed me as to why Green Scales is here today, and if what she says is true, we should all listen."

After that, I shared your warning about allying ourselves with Cicia, carefully hiding how you knew such things. All I said was that you were from Cicia and had connections with reliable informants. Numa frowned again a little, and others glanced at each other, but the oddness of your attire convinced everyone that *someone like you* would indeed have shady connections.

Jovien didn't argue. He had never liked the prospect of

allying ourselves with Cicia. It had been my idea, and he had followed it because we had no alternative at the time. Now we had the alternative he longed for in the form of three miraculous suits you displayed to him and others. You explained how they worked, unminiaturizing one after the other. While Jovien kept his usual composure and only nodded to express himself, Vark's behavior had shifted to awe. Numa, too, seemed intrigued by the suits—almost scared of them, as if they were powerful but dangerous things. Your miniaturizer intrigued him, too. He had probably never seen a portable one before. It was a rare, expensive device only few people possessed in the galaxy.

Once you were done introducing the Cician technology that was now ours, I explained our plan. "Instead of storming the governor's manor and fighting our way in, we'll be stealthy. We'll strike shortly before eleven in the evening, an hour before the changing of the guard. The guards will be tired and less attentive. One of us will use the moon-suit to climb the outer wall and unlock the side gate, then let others in. Another will use the time-suit to disarm the guards, tie and gag them, and give their weapons to other Bronzees. I want the guards to be unharmed, so don't use their weapons against them unless you truly have no choice. Let's not have any bloodshed." I turned to Vark. "At the same time, I'll need you to go door-to-door and tell our supporters in the city, so they can demonstrate in the streets and rally at the mansion as we escort the governor to the cell where he belongs. I want him to see that this isn't a coup. It's a revolution."

"Vark fights better than I do," Numa said. "It would be best to have him at the mansion. I can rally our people."

A fair point, but I said, "Vark knows more people. He was born and raised in Prophis. If *he* believes we're about to succeed, people will believe and follow him. Also, I have another assignment for you that I will share in time."

Numa nodded, disappointed but understanding. You, more than others, understood his reluctance to be at the forefront of the action. You planned to join us, as you wanted to do everything possible to ensure our success, but still dreaded the confrontation with armed guards, regardless of our ability to disarm them quickly.

"When should we strike?" Vark asked.

I opened my mouth to answer, but you whispered in my ear, "Don't tell them—for the same reason you don't tell them the meeting time and location in advance."

You were right. If one of us suddenly had cold feet and betrayed us to the governor, we would run right into a trap.

"Jovien and I will discuss it," I said, "and we'll tell you when we have chosen the best moment. But before that, I need to confirm we're in agreement with this new plan. We won't ally ourselves with Cicia, and we will follow the plan I just laid out. If you have questions, ask them now."

After they asked questions that you and I answered the best we could, Jovien passed down small pieces of paper and pens, inviting everyone to cast their vote, and collected the ballots in a wooden basket. Then Jovien and I added our votes. You didn't participate, of course. You were not a Bronzee. Not officially, even if to me, you were already one of us.

"Eleven votes for the new plan, two against it," Jovien said once he and I finished counting. He cleared his throat. "I understand how some of you are skeptical and believe we should stick to the first one, but you know the rule. The majority has agreed to the new plan, so we will proceed with it. Are you *all* in agreement? Raise your hand if you understand."

Everybody raised their hand. It was only for form, but still important. We had to confirm everyone committed to the collective decision we had taken, regardless of individual disagreements.

I concluded the meeting shortly afterward, both hopeful and wary about the future. I knew we could succeed, but I also knew the price of defeat. If we failed, life in prison awaited the Bronzees. Jovien would be excluded from his temple, and I would go back to the winter palace—locked in a room, this time—if I weren't executed right away. As for you, imagining what your capture meant was too painful. It could start a war if the emperor accused you of destabilizing the empire for Cicia's profit before throwing you into a cell. And if Elias peacefully negotiated your release, you would have no choice but to marry him. I couldn't let that happen.

The Bronzees left one by one as they had come, Jovien last. Before climbing the stairs, he put on a long coat over his robe and passed his hand across his face to alter his features, making you gasp. You had heard about Cleansers' abilities and how they could take multiple faces in the image of their god, but it was disturbing to see the change before your eyes. How convenient it would have been for you to possess the same ability. The illusion wasn't perfect, but perhaps you wouldn't have had to wear a mask all the time.

Once he was gone, I turned to you and said, "I received news from your mother."

"When?" you asked precipitately while moving toward me, a hand over your fast-beating heart. "Is she fine?"

"Yesterday evening. My contact's envoy visited her temple in Hyla three Therrian days ago. Your mother was still there. She looked fine. Shaken, for sure. He asked her for a serening ritual and told her during the spirit-bond that you were safe. We didn't tell the envoy where you were on Phau to make sure she couldn't know by glimpsing into his mind. I know how important it is that she doesn't know your exact location."

You exhaled loudly, relieved. "What did she say?" you asked, your voice trembling a little. "Did she send back a message?"

"Only that she loves you and hopes to see you again."

You fought back the tears coming to your eyes, then you whispered, "Thank you."

I nodded and said the only thing I could think of. "I'm glad I could help." It probably came out as lame as I thought it sounded, but you still smiled. It was such a big smile that, despite not seeing your lips moving under your mask, I saw it in your eyes.

Then you approached me, and without asking, you hugged me. My heart pounded in my chest as your body touched mine, and I didn't know what to do with my own arms. Should I hug you back? But what if I held you too tight, not wanting to let you go? I would make a fool of myself—*again*. So instead I waited for you to end the unexpected embrace, feeling both happy and stupid for my inability to respond to your gesture.

At last, you moved away and said, before climbing the stairs, "You are an eloquent woman, Sianna, and a kind one, too."

I watched you go and knew I wanted you to join not only our revolution, but also my life.

SIXTHDAY 18 SUMMUCIEL 1497 AE
PROPHIS, ETHILIAN EMPIRE COLONY, PHAU

What is happening to me? Why did I feel the urge to embrace Sianna? A simple thank-you would have been enough, yet I couldn't help but want to hold her in my arms.

I do feel unexpected feelings for her, and I don't believe these are merely caused by remnants of the spirit-bond. Her poise, her passion, her empathy (I can't believe she actually contacted Mother for me!), her endurance, her leader-ship . . . she is everything I wish I were, but I am not jealous. I don't want to be her. I want to be with her.

If it wasn't for Sianna, I wouldn't have joined the Bronze Faction. But they sincerely believe they can make Prophis a better place and have a solid plan to do so. I can't believe the emperor will let Prophis be free willingly, just as I can't believe Elias would ever give up his crown. The Bronze Faction will have to fight for Prophis's freedom, and I'll be fighting with them.

WHILE I WORKED with Jovien on the details of our plan, you kept working in the kitchen as if nothing had changed. When you weren't working, you kept searching for the ideal spawning location for the eggs, clinging to the hope that Prophis and the surrounding region would soon be free of both the emperor's grip and your brother's covetousness, ensuring the young snakes wouldn't become captive like their mother. You made good progress, identifying multiple suitable locations, and you even planned on telling me about the eggs once the governor wasn't in charge anymore.

I had always looked forward to my lunch break. Driving a forklift in the storehouse wasn't as exhausting as mining—I'd asked the boss to let me get my certification for a reason—but my back always ached after sitting all day. And now, going to the cafeteria also meant seeing you. The morning could never pass fast enough.

Numa grew closer to you, pairing up with you in the kitchen whenever Trizia allowed it. He was eager to know you better, but you were still reluctant to share anything about your past, and while he said he understood, you could see the frustration behind his gentle smiles. Vark's behavior changed, too. He wasn't as friendly as Numa, but his politeness improved and influenced the attitude of other miners. The teasing ceased, and soon you were barely getting any sidelong glances or rude comments. Prophis had truly become your home, and you were ready to defend it from Cicia on the day I shared a coded message in the cafeteria between two bites of steamed fish.

"I'd like to invite you to a purification ritual at the temple tonight," I said softly. "There'll be a grand ceremony, with beautiful costumes. A purification ritual like no other, where Brother Jovien will prepare Ystos's followers for challenges to come."

I worried it was too vague, but you nodded and asked, leaning toward me, "At what time should I come to the temple?"

"At dusk," I whispered in your ear.

You nodded again. "I will be there."

At this time of the year, the sun set before nine in the evening, barely an hour later than during winter. It left you time to prepare yourself. Tonight could bring hope to a world riddled with power-hungry men who only cared about colonizing exoplanets and expanding their influence. You surprised yourself with how much you cared about it. Not only because you had to protect Prophis from Cicia for your sake and that of Celadon's children, but because you finally had a chance to choose for yourself. You were done with following the path traced by your birth and by your brother. Done fleeing. Tonight, you would make your stand among us, choosing to side with the people and with yourself.

In your room, you carefully placed the miniaturized eggs in your cache. You couldn't risk them being caught with you in case things went wrong. After whispering a prayer to Zephis to protect them in your absence, you said, "I haven't forgotten my promise. Celadon's children are growing, and soon I will bring them to a place where they can be born." You had learned that the diastium vein exploited in Prophis stretched for dozens of miles underground, all the way to New Zankia, where Celadon's children could thrive. All you had to do was follow the maps now in your possession, thanks again to the books Numa had brought you from the library. But first, Prophis had to become a free city.

Shortly before dusk, you went to the Temple of Purity. Jovien waited near the entrance. Seeing him standing in front of the temple reminded you of your mother waiting for you on the day Elias gave you the time-suit. The day you committed blasphemy and asked for Celadon's death in Zephis's name. *I can't think about that now,* you told yourself, chasing the memory away. You had to focus on the present moment.

Jovien wasn't wearing his priest attire. Instead, he wore a close-fitting black outfit similar to the one you wore under your snake-suit, which meant he planned to use one of the three suits. Not only was he the Faction's founder and obviously willing to fight tonight, but his stature was similar to yours, so it didn't surprise you. He was only a little taller than you. The suits would fit him well.

After giving you a nod, he escorted you through the gate. The temple's layout was similar to that of the Temple of Serenity in Hyla, except for the pond in the center of the courtyard, around which we were all seated, waiting for you. You noticed that Vark and I wore close-fitting outfits, too.

Your arrival lifted a weight off my mind. You had come. You had been true to your word.

As you sat among us, Jovien explained how the pond was filled with rainwater only—Ystos's blessing—and infused with the god's cleansing strength, which he would use for the ritual before the Faction moved to action. It surprised you; you hadn't expected the ritual to actually happen. But Jovien was a devout man, and it made sense to ask for Ystos's blessing. When you asked about the High Priestess and other Cleansers living in the temple, he gave you a reassuring smile that made you understand they were all complicit. You smiled back at him. I hadn't lied when I told you Prophisians were behind the Faction. Cleansers had helped us build the popular support we needed to be successful, and the High Priestess herself would make a powerful ally during the transition period that would follow tonight's revolution.

Jovien distributed silver cups and instructed us to fill them with water from the pond. You watched the others do it first before imitating us. The water in the cup was pristine and had a scent reminiscent of the roses that flourished in the gardens of Hyla's palace. It eerily distorted the three-face engraving at the bottom of the cup, sending a shiver down your spine, as if Ystos's six eyes were upon you. You didn't know what to do with the water, so you kept holding the cup, watching Jovien in anticipation.

"Ystos's blessing nourishes our spirit like it nourishes the earth," he said in a solemn tone. "It cleanses corruption in our heart, and tonight it will cleanse the corruption that took root in our city. Drink, my brothers and sisters, and feel Ystos's blessing enter your body and warm your spirit."

You lowered your head, moved your hood to better hide your face, and lifted your mask just enough to bring the cup to your lips. Before you could take a sip, I touched your arm and whispered, "Drink slowly." Your enthusiasm to drink had told me you had never attended a purification ritual. If I had let you gulp down the water, you would have suffered an experience more painful than a forced spirit-bond.

So you drank slowly, one sip after the other, letting the blessed water fill your body with a strength you had never felt before. The water brought terrible thoughts to your mind—your blasphemy first, then every moment of your life where you had committed a spirit-tainting deed—but as soon as the thoughts came, the water washed them away. By accepting Ystos's blessing, you cleansed yourself and readied your spirit for honorable deeds. The more you drank, the better you felt, and the last sip made you want to put the governor in jail yourself.

"As long as you act with justice in mind, Ystos will be with you," Jovien said. "He does not tolerate corruption and injustice from anyone, not even from the other gods themselves. But tonight, the corruption we seek to cleanse is very human."

His speech over, Jovien whispered a prayer to Ystos, asking for the god's blessing. A dark cloud formed above Prophis as he recited the prayer, and soon a light rain began falling upon the city. Vark gasped in wonder and said that Ystos had heard us and was sanctifying our mission. With a god on our side, nothing would stop the Faction tonight.

Jovien and I exchanged confident smiles before asking Vark, Numa, and you to follow us inside the temple's building. There, we asked you for the suits. Jovien had volunteered to use the moon-suit and infiltrate the mansion first, then open the gate for all of us to follow. I would wear the time-suit and take care of disarming the guards. Once the gardens were clear of danger, Numa would sneak to the electrical cabinet inside a shed nobody guarded and cut the power, disabling important security mechanisms to allow the rest of the group to progress in the mansion without triggering alarms. As for Vark, he would use the sun-suit to gather people in the city like a guiding light, starting with the mine's housing building, where the workers had been ready for a revolution since their first breath.

As we were putting the suits over our clothes, you gave me a concerned look, and I saw in your eyes that you worried about my safety. I would take the most dangerous role, but I had chosen it, I told you. Jovien and I agreed that as the Faction's leaders, it was our responsibility to take the greatest risks. It didn't make you feel better, but you understood.

"What about *my* role?" you asked.

Your three suits are enough, I wanted to say, but kept to myself. I knew you would ask and wouldn't take no for an answer, so Jovien and I had included you in our plan.

"You're coming with us," I said, before taking you aside and telling you how you could help. Not only would you increase our numbers, but your miniaturizer would help us carry anything valuable we could find in the mansion. Documents. Weapons. Imperial technology. If the need arose, you would use your abilities to serene reluctant guards into submission, erasing their will to fight us.

The assignment satisfied you, and you followed us back to the pond, where Jovien and I gave each Bronzee their assignment. I could feel their nervousness, and so could you. The purification ritual had lifted their spirits, but not altered their reason. They knew tonight might be their last.

The sun had set already and the cloud still poured rain over the city when we left the temple and marched toward the governor's mansion.

WALKING IN THE time-suit felt like wandering in my own dreams. Everything around me was eerily slower, as if I were in one of the mirages tricking inexperienced travelers in the savanna, except everything around me was real and not a fading illusion.

So, once I got used to the uncomfortable feeling, I walked onto the mansion grounds like I was walking into a dream. I neutralized the two guards posted near the side gate with disconcerting ease, then grabbed their weapons and put them in the hands of two Bronzees in a matter of what must have been a second for you and the others. Their wrists were tied together and their mouths gagged before they had time to recover from their slumber. Then Jovien used the moon-suit to jump to the top of the outer wall and carefully land on the other side. Once he unlocked the gate, we entered silently and moved toward the governor's apartment in the south wing of the mansion.

I was tempted to run ahead of everyone to the governor's bedroom, but it would have been suicide. The time-suit wouldn't protect me against a horde of guards shooting at me and gods-know-what security systems we weren't already aware of. Diaston was bulletproof, but not a super-natural shield. The impact of high velocity bullets would still hurt my body under the suit. So I stuck to our plan and progressed in the mansion step-by-step, guard after guard, door after door, always ensuring you and other Bronzees followed me closely.

Only once did I ask you to use your powers to calm a guard. Perhaps I didn't tie his wrists well enough or he was stronger than the others. You established the spirit-bond and serened him as gently as you could, taking away his worries and his will to protect the governor. A glimpse into his mind showed you a man who believed he was only doing his job, a job he neither loved nor hated. He disliked the governor's bad temper but appreciated offering a comfortable life to his family, thanks to the generous pay— pay he didn't realize was high only because others in the city were exploited or overtaxed. Of course, he would be upset at failing at his job and losing his livelihood. He feared being fired, or worse, executed in the case of the governor being killed. You soothed him, reassuring him that no one would die tonight, and soon he fell into a peaceful reverie.

I had told Jovien about your Serenitress training, and if he guessed your identity, he didn't tell me and he didn't betray your secret either. When other Bronzees asked how you had calmed the guard so easily, Jovien told them Green

Scales had many skills and reminded them to stay focused.

At last, we reached the door leading to the governor's apartment. There were no guards here, because the door itself was heavy and secured. Forcing it would trigger an alarm in the governor's bedroom so he could escape to safety. Thankfully, one of the workers who had installed the security mechanism was also a devout follower of Ystos, and had confided to Jovien that without power, the alarm wouldn't ring. All we had to do was pull the plug in the electrical cabinet.

We were ready to break into the apartment, but the lights were still on. I glanced at Jovien's watch—mine wasn't accurate since I had used the time-suit. Numa should have already reached the shed and cut off the power. Had he unexpectedly run into a guard and been captured? But we would have heard the commotion. The guard would have called for help. No, Numa was probably a little late, that was it.

In silence, we waited. After five minutes that felt like an hour, Jovien handed me his goggles, and I walked to a window overlooking the gardens. I saw the shed, but couldn't tell if Numa was already inside. He wasn't outside. The only guards I spotted stood beyond the outer wall, in front of the main gate. They were too far from the shed to see or hear Numa and looked engaged in a lively conversation, unaware of the situation inside the mansion.

"What are you doing, Numa?" I whispered to myself.

"We can't afford to wait much longer," Jovien said.

Another Bronzee, a young woman named Eulia who worked in Prophis's port, approached me and said, "Jovien is right, Sianna. The longer we wait, the more likely we are to get spotted. If a patrol walks by the side gate and notices nobody's guarding it—"

"I'll go," I said. "I'll use the time-suit again and flip that damn switch myself."

Before I could press the button to speed up time, you touched my arm and whispered in my ear, "It could be dangerous." Despite the voice-warping device distorting your tone, I heard your concern. "What if he has been caught and guards are waiting for you?"

I gave you a smile that I wanted to be reassuring, but that manifested itself as strained and hesitant. I said, "He hasn't been caught. There are no guards in that part of the mansion."

You squeezed my arm tighter. "Sianna, please. You could be wrong."

"I have no choice," I said, before conceding, "but I'll be careful. I promise. I'll be back in a few seconds."

Reluctantly, you let me go.

I sped up time again, twice as fast as before. You had warned me against overusing the suit's powers, but we couldn't wait any longer. I retraced our steps to the building's entrance. Outside, the rain had stopped, and rain crickets filled the air with their song. Everyone in Prophis loved the crickets' song, for it came only after Ystos had blessed the city. I loved it too, but the time distortion changed it into a slow and scary melody made of shrilling sounds.

I moved carefully toward the shed, looking around for guards. There shouldn't be any, but what if I was wrong, like you said? But the gardens were empty. I couldn't see a single soul, and though it should have reassured me, it didn't. Where was Numa? Were the gardens empty because guards had captured him and taken him away? I shivered. Numa, at the mercy of the governor's men. Numa, in a cell. Numa, being interrogated. No, I couldn't imagine one of my Bronzees subjected to such a terrible fate. And not Numa.

He was strong and resourceful. I had assigned him this mission because he was capable. I wouldn't have trusted anyone else more than him. But finding the shed locked only reinforced my concern. The lock was simple. Nothing Numa couldn't pick. My heart beating fast in my chest, I looked around again, half expecting to see a shadow jump at me, but nothing happened.

I sighed. I wished I had time to look for Numa, but I didn't. All I could hope for was that he had actually escaped and found a place to hide. Like all Bronzees, he knew that being captured was the worst that could happen during a mission. Worse than failing the mission itself. Removing a hairpin from my hair, I picked the lock and walked inside the shed. It was empty, too. Quickly, I opened the electrical cabinet and pointed my flashlight to the circuit breakers, looking for the one controlling power in the south wing.

"Found you," I whispered as I switched the breaker.

I glanced outside of the shed toward the window where I had been looking for Numa through Jovien's goggles a moment ago. The lights were out. Good.

As I went back inside the mansion, I found myself silently praying to Ystos for Numa to be safe. I wasn't pious, but stress always made me turn to the gods for help, and tonight was the most stressful night I had ever lived.

I slowed down time to normal speed as soon as I reached you.

"You are back," you said, as if you wanted to reinforce a reality you had feared would not happen.

I gestured at the surrounding darkness and said, "And successful." I glanced at my watch. From my perspective, I had left you six minutes ago, but to you, it had been less than a half minute.

"What about Numa?" Jovien asked. "Did you find him?"

I shook my head, a knot in my stomach. "I don't know where he is. Captured, maybe."

Jovien walked to the window and pointed his goggles at the two guards standing at the main gate. "Then why are the guards unalarmed?"

"I don't know," I whispered. "Maybe they didn't see us and thought he was alone."

Eulia clicked her tongue and shook her head in disbelief. "The whole mansion was on alert only five seconds after a guard saw Vark and me on the night of our failed burglary. Numa must've freaked out and fled, that's it."

"No," I said firmly. "He wouldn't do that."

"Perhaps he betrayed us."

I froze. *You* were the one who had said that. After everything Numa had done for you, I couldn't believe you were accusing him of betrayal.

"Betrayed us," I said, turning to you, "to the governor?"

"I don't know," you whispered, troubled by my displeased tone. "He didn't like our new plan. Then he wanted Vark's role. Perhaps—"

"Vark is arriving with a large crowd," Jovien said, interrupting you with a deep, commanding voice. He pointed at the window, where we all saw a glowing light moving toward the mansion's main gate. "We can't debate any longer. We need to catch the governor now and incapacitate the two guards at the gate."

"If Numa betrayed us—"

"Which he didn't," I snapped impatiently, interrupting Eulia.

"If he betrayed us," she repeated, "then the governor is probably gone already and we're walking into a trap."

"Eulia is right," another Bronzee said while two others nodded behind him.

"Only one way to find out," I said as I walked to the door. "Give me your crowbar, Eulia. I'll open it myself. Stay behind if you're worried."

Eulia nodded slowly before tossing her crowbar at me. I grabbed it and forced the door. As soon as it moved, I walked inside the governor's apartment, glancing over my shoulder to check who was following. Jovien was right behind me, and behind him was you. You gave me a reassuring look that meant *I am still with you*, lifting my spirit. Eulia muttered something under her breath before following us, and soon the other Bronzees imitated her.

Three more doors—unlocked, this time—stood between us and the governor. We moved as discreetly as we could, until we reached the bedroom and found the governor half awake in his bed, a baffled expression appearing on his face as he saw me. He hadn't known we were coming. Numa hadn't betrayed us.

"It's over, Madorin," I said, refusing to call him by a title he didn't deserve.

"You," he spat, recognizing me. "You, of all the people in this blasted city!"

"Seize him," I ordered.

After that, everything happened quickly. I had so much adrenaline flowing in my body that I felt disconnected from reality, and I remember what happened only because your presence anchored me, keeping me focused on the task at hand.

Jovien and Eulia immobilized the governor while I hand-cuffed him, ignoring the torrent of insults and threats he poured at me. I didn't silence him when he called me by my full name. Everyone but you and Jovien stared at me, their eyes filled with a blend of amazement and disbelief, and I could already imagine Vark's reaction when he learned that Sianna the Bronzee was *the* Lady Avasiannata. I didn't care about being anonymous anymore. We had succeeded, and I couldn't wait for the emperor to learn that *I* had deprived him of Prophis.

We escorted the governor outside the mansion and moved toward the main gate. I couldn't help but look for Numa as we walked through the gardens, a pang of guilt filling my chest. I almost hoped he got scared and abandoned us. I'd rather he be a coward than a dead man. But I didn't have time to worry about Numa, because Vark was about to reach the gate, the crowd behind him so loud that I could barely hear the rain crickets' song. The two guards still standing at the main gate tried to call for reinforcements, but no one responded to their calls, and soon they looked behind and saw us and the governor. I didn't need to ask them to surrender. Cornered and outnumbered, their mission to protect the governor failed already, they dropped their weapons and stayed quiet as I tied their wrists.

"You will regret it," the governor hissed at me.

"Perhaps, but Prophis won't regret deposing *you*," I said, gesturing toward the chanting crowd that was already encircling us.

"Take him to the prison!" Vark said, manipulating the sun-suit's controls to shine a little more.

The crowd roared. I held my breath. The rain crickets sang louder.

And in the middle of the chaos, you kissed me.

V

Yes, I know what you're thinking. You have been listening carefully to your own story. I see it in your intense look and in your smiles. I hear it when you gasp when I tell you the incredible things that happened to you, to us. I know speaking is difficult for you, after so much time away from civilization and in your state. I don't mind doing most of the talking, my love.

So where was I? I know why you doubt my words. Surely I was the one initiating the kiss. You still had to keep your identity secret. You couldn't possibly have removed your snake-mask and showed your face to everyone to press your lips against mine. That would be foolish, and you weren't a fool. But I swear, you did it.

MY HEART EXPLODED like a supernova as the softness of your lips filled my body and mind with the warmth of a star. I was so shocked and so still that it felt like lightning had struck me.

After a moment that felt like an eternity, you pulled away and stared at me silently. A glimpse of fear flashed in your eyes. The fear that I actually didn't want you, that you had been wrong to kiss me. I silently cursed myself and my inability to react, until I finally found the strength to move. Before you could step away any farther, my arms were around you and my mouth pressing against yours, dispelling your fears. I pulled you closer and closed my eyes, tasting the sweet softness of your lips once again and already knowing I would desire them for the rest of my life. You were mine, and I was yours, and no king or emperor or governor would pull us apart. Not even the gods, if you can forgive my blasphemy.

Neither you nor I cared that everyone saw us. We didn't care about the rumors of the runaway princess kissing the leader of the rebellion—who was none other than the emperor's stepdaughter—that would spread in the morning. We had freed Prophis. The city was ours. We wouldn't let anyone take it back from us.

We didn't sleep that night. The morning would hit us with the enormous task of organizing Prophis's future, but now was the time to celebrate our victory. The crowd led by Vark escorted the governor to his own prison, surprisingly not harming him in the process. Perhaps our unexpected kiss had soothed the angry crowd.

In his night garments, without guards to point deadly weapons at us, the governor was a pitiful old man who couldn't hurt us no matter how much he wanted it. Oh, he still had supporters in the city. People loyal to the empire who would manifest themselves sooner or later to attempt freeing him. Soon, we would find and exile them. But tonight they hid.

While other citizens celebrated, we slipped away to my place, a small haven on the top floor of an old brick building perched on the top of a hill. You weren't the first woman I had brought back home for the night, but you were the first since I had escaped the winter palace and settled in Prophis. I had been too preoccupied with the Faction to allow myself time to love anything else but my ideals. But you changed everything. Not only did you allow me to free Prophis, but now you also allowed me to free myself from my obsessions, if only for one night, hopefully for many more.

There have been, to my delight, many more nights, but I wish you could remember that one. It pains me to know you have forgotten such an intense and joyful moment. My hands brushing your alabaster skin, my mouth devouring your body and spirit, your silvery voice begging me to never stop. I don't blame you, of course. I know the memory is still there, deep down inside your mind, and that you will recover it. That's why I'm telling you your story, you see? I know I'm defying a goddess by doing so. I'm defying your goddess, but I told you: No one can pull us apart. Not even Zephis herself. And I have the blessing of another god. I wouldn't have come all the way into the savanna if Ystos himself hadn't given me the means to free you after I spent countless nights praying and convincing him of the unfairness of your predicament. Of the corruption of your very soul, caused by a goddess too eager to punish those who displease her, even if they do it for a just cause. But you need to remember, first. If you don't remember, the blessed water won't work. I need you to

remember me, to remember us, and most importantly, to remember yourself.

"THERE IS SOMETHING I need to show you," you said as the first sunbeams pierced through the clouds above the Auriverian Sea.

"What is it?" I asked.

"It's in my room," you said, before getting up and dressing in your snake-suit. I quickly put clothes on too, eager to find out more. "The reason I found refuge on Phau and not another planet."

As we stepped outside, all my worries about Prophis's future came back at once. The city was under control thanks to the High Priestess, who had dispatched her priests and priestesses across the city to maintain peace, but I still felt like an inevitable doom was about to come down on us. On our way to the mine, we crossed paths with Eulia and a young priest patrolling the commercial district. I asked them if Numa had appeared at the temple during the night, but they both shook their heads, tightening the knot that was growing in my stomach.

We found the mine operating as if nothing had happened. The boss wasn't there anymore, and employees had organized themselves to keep mining diastium. Vark was behind this, of course. He had spent years preparing the Faction's loyalists for the day we would free Prophis from the empire. The boss hadn't dared show up, knowing he would be kicked out the moment he set foot inside the mine's premises—if not thrown inside a cell alongside the governor. The diastium was ours and wouldn't power the empire's fleet anymore.

Your hands began to shake once you'd inserted the key to open your room's door. It should have been locked, but the key didn't budge as you tried turning it. The door was unlocked already. Your heart beating fast inside your chest, you pushed the door open, and a scream died inside your throat as you saw your room turned upside down.

"No," you whispered while staring at your bed. Its frame and mattress had been shoved across the room. You moved your eyes to the floor. The slate hiding your cache was destroyed. You rushed to the cache, dropped to your knees, and searched frantically for the miniaturized eggs, but it was empty. The eggs were gone. You had failed Celadon. You had failed your goddess. *One more time.*

"Someone stole them," you said matter-of-factly. Your voice was cold, your eyes dry. You had already cried all the tears you could shed. "Zephis will never forgive me."

"Someone stole what, Cyrelle?" I asked quietly, as if not to offend the goddess myself.

"The eggs. Celadon's children. Someone took them," you continued, speaking flatly, factually, your mind visibly racing with thoughts. "Someone who knew about them and about my miniaturizer. Someone who knew they could look like green marbles. I left them miniaturized in my cache."

I gave you a half-worried, half-inquisitive gaze, and you told me everything about Celadon, the eggs, and Zephis's vision. I listened quietly, absorbing the information and trying not to let myself be submerged in my emotions. Amazement. Frustration, too. Why hadn't you told me sooner? I could have helped you protect the eggs! Now they were gone, and who knew what punishment your goddess would deem suitable for such a failure?

But the most pressing question that burned your lips was "How did my brother find me?" Even if Prophisians had recognized you when we kissed each other yesterday, and somehow word had reached Elias, how could he have sent someone so quickly? No, it was impossible. He knew already and had waited for the right time to retrieve the eggs.

"Numa," I whispered, incredulous.

Your eyes opened wide with understanding, and together, we rushed to his room. It was unlocked and *empty*.

"How?" I asked, mostly to myself. How had I missed that Numa wasn't as loyal as he pretended? How did he manipulate me and Jovien into believing he cared about the city? He had been so convincing, so devoted to the cause. I couldn't believe it had been a deception, yet I couldn't deny the pieces falling into place in front of my eyes. It couldn't be a coincidence, no matter how hard I wished it was.

There was only one logical explanation. Numa hadn't been captured, and he hadn't betrayed us to the empire. He had betrayed us to *Cicia*. Since we hadn't told him who you were, that meant only one thing: He knew about the suits. The moment we showed them to the Faction, he recognized you, because he had been working for Cicia since the beginning. He wasn't a traitor, for he had always been loyal to one cause only. He was an undercover Cician agent. All that time since I had joined the Bronze Faction, I had feared the presence of an Ethilian spy, someone who would turn me in to my stepfather and ruin my plan to take Prophis away from his grasp. I had never considered the threat could come from another country.

I didn't have to explain any of it, because you figured it out yourself, saying out loud what I struggled to believe.

"Numa worked for my brother," you said, before telling me how Elias had surely tasked Numa to infiltrate the Faction and influence us to strike an agreement with Cicia, only to change plans the moment he learned Numa had found you. The alliance between the Faction and Cicia didn't matter anymore. He had coveted the mine for years, and more than ever after you fled with the eggs, but finding you had made him reconsider his plan. The eggs were more important than Prophis and its rebels. So he asked Numa to find them, and Numa took advantage of your absence to search your room. The eggs found, he had no business in Prophis anymore, and Elias called him back. "No wonder why he wanted Vark's role last night," you spat. "He wasn't afraid. He wanted a valid excuse to not be with us at the governor's mansion."

I nodded, forced to admit we had both been duped by a man we thought to be our friend. You, for several months. Me and Jovien, for *years*, and we saw *nothing*. We had succeeded in overthrowing the governor, yet Numa's deception made me feel like an utter failure. How could I have missed it for all this time?

This could have been the end of it, but deep down, something told us it wasn't over. Elias may have retrieved the eggs, but his greed wouldn't stop there. He might still want to take Prophis, and most dreadfully, he might still want *you*.

"I won't let him take you," I said, my voice trembling. Could I really protect you from Elias? I didn't know, but I wanted to believe it. You could hide inside the temple. We could dress you as a Cleanser, give you a false name, hide your face with the veil Ystos's apprentices wear until they take their vows.

But you shook your head and said, "You don't understand, Sianna. He has Celadon's children. I must retrieve them. I must go back to him."

"No," I said, louder than expected. "Cyrelle, you can't—"

"But he will *not* have me," you said firmly as you took my

hands and brought them close to your chest. "I will make him think that he can have it all—the eggs, the city, the marriage—but I promise you, Sianna, that he will have *nothing*."

FIRSTDAY 1 PRIMIFALL 1497 AE
PROPHIS, ETHILIAN EMPIRE COLONY, PHAU

Sianna didn't believe me when I said Elias would have nothing. She thinks it is insane for me to go back to my brother to retrieve the eggs. Thankfully she understands why they matter, but she still believes the risk is too high.

Tomorrow, I meet with my brother's puppet, and if he deigns to appear, with Elias himself. I will plead, I will apologize, I will throw myself at his feet if I have to, but it will only be a façade. He will expect a meek princess begging for forgiveness, he will believe he has the upper hand, but he doesn't know how much I have changed during the past months. I am not the Cyrelle I used to be. I am not even Green Scales. I don't need her anymore. I am done hiding under a snakeskin or under suits that can't actually change who I am. Time changed me, and now Elias will reap what he sowed the day he decided he would make me his queen.

I will never hide who I am again.

THE NEXT DAY, you put your sun-suit on and went to the harbor where Cicia's emissary was expecting you. I wish I could have come with you, but your plan didn't allow it. So instead, I asked Eulia to follow you from afar and immediately alert me if you didn't emerge from the warehouse where the meeting would happen. I had plenty of work to do in Prophis—emissaries from concerned foreign states to meet and reassure of our good will, imperialists to expel from the city, free elections to organize—but all I could think about was you.

You walked through the city with your chin up, drawing curious looks from everyone who crossed your path. The runaway princess had found refuge in Prophis and had helped the Faction liberate the city! Rumors were already spreading through the streets like an unstoppable wind. Some believed we had been fostering a long-distance relationship, and you had fled the wedding because you wanted to be with me. Others wondered if your brother had sent you to Prophis to seduce me so Cicia could seize the city later. None of the rumors were true, but you were grateful for them, especially the ones that implied your allegiance to Cicia, because that's exactly what you wanted the emissary and your brother to believe.

"Your Highness," the emissary said as you entered the warehouse.

You squinted at him, recognizing his features but unable to remember his name. A distant cousin on your father's side, you astutely assumed, because he said, "I am Lord Hamidas," and you remembered visiting his family's mansion on Therria many years ago. He was about your age, and must have been among those who had teased you about your mother's modest origins before he grew out of it. That he had become an emissary on Phau didn't surprise you. Assigning high-ranking positions to the extended royal family ensured their wealth and consequential loyalty.

"I don't have much time," you said very fast. "Lady Avasiannata will become suspicious if I absent myself for too long. It was already difficult to contact you without her knowing."

"I understand," he replied tersely.

"I nee—I *must* speak to my brother immediately." You didn't want to sound desperate, and you were a princess, after all. A princess doesn't plead with emissaries. She states what she wants, and she gets it.

Lord Hamidas nodded and placed a holophone on the floor. "After what happened, Your Highness surely under-stands that His Majesty couldn't take the risk of coming in person."

You snorted. You hadn't expected to see Elias in the flesh, but you were still disappointed by his lack of courage. "As long as I can talk to him. Alone."

"I am afraid the instructions I received from His Majesty don't allow me to leave until the conversation is over."

You opened your mouth to argue, but reconsidered. "Very well. Initiate the holocall."

Lord Hamidas pressed the holophone. A few seconds later, the image of Elias appeared above the device. He observed you for an instant before saying, "Don't you look radiant."

You recognized the *Lifebringer*'s communication room. He hadn't bothered landing on the planet. "Elias," you answered. A tense smile twisted your lips. "It is a relief to talk to you."

"Is it?" His voice was low, and his tone was on the verge of sarcasm. "Mother's memories showed the opposite. You seemed adamant about never seeing me again."

You gulped, doing your best not to scream as you understood the implication of his last sentence. He had pressured the Temple of Serenity into subjecting your mother to a forced spirit-bond to explore her memories. Your mother was good at fighting unwanted spirit-bonds and must have concealed the most compromising memories, but who knew what Elias had learned? You wanted to spit at the foot of his hologram for daring to commit such an outrageous act against your goddess—and, by the gods, against *his own mother*—but restrained yourself. "Fleeing was a mistake," you said softly, looking down. "You know I love you, but when I sought advice from our mother, she convinced me it was an unnatural union. I let her words poison my mind and corrupt the feelings I had for you." You raised your gaze and looked him in the eye. "I only understood it recently, after the weight of your absence became unbearable."

You glanced at Lord Hamidas, who looked away. He was doing his best to keep his composure, but you easily noticed his embarrassment. You couldn't blame him. The extended royal family's loyalty to Elias didn't prevent them from mocking his behavior in private, and the incestuous marriage proposal must have given them enough to gossip about for an entire decade.

Elias snorted. "Even if I believed you, you still stole from me, Cyrelle. I had hoped to be wrong about it, but my agent found what was mine *in your room.*"

The eggs. "None of that would have been necessary if I had known Numa's true allegiance," you said. "I would have gladly returned the eggs to you."

"Is that so?" he asked, frowning in disbelief.

You pressed your lips together. Elias wasn't going to trust you blindly. At least you were now absolutely certain that he had the eggs. "I never wanted Celadon to die. Neither did Zephis. It was Mother's idea." You silently cursed yourself for putting the blame on your mother, but you had no choice. Elias had to trust you, and nothing would happen to her. You would make sure of that. "For my lie, Zephis punished me by charging me with the task of taking the eggs to Phau."

"And you obeyed her, putting the entire kingdom's future in jeopardy."

"I was terrified," you said with a pleading voice. "I lied about the first vision, but after you had Celadon executed, Zephis sent me a *real* vision ordering me to take the eggs to Phau to atone for my sin. What would you do if Eterion did the same to you? Wouldn't you obey him?"

He didn't respond.

"I want to come back," you said after the silence had become too uncomfortable. "I want to come back, marry you, and raise Celadon's children alongside you. We could build a serpentarium on Phau, so I can keep my promise to Zephis *and* we can harvest the shed skins."

He raised an eyebrow. He was still unconvinced, but you were making progress.

"I even have a nuptial gift, which you deserve after the gifts you gave me already." You gestured toward your sunsuit so as to reinforce your point.

"A nuptial gift," he whispered with a slightly curious tone.

You smiled. You definitely knew how to appeal to your brother. "Prophis." You let the word sink into his mind for a few seconds before continuing, "I am close to Lady Avasiannata. She trusts me. I could easily manipulate her to do something in our interest."

"Lord Hamidas was already working on that," he said, glancing at the emissary, "and I heard that *you* ruined our efforts."

You clicked your tongue. "With all due respect to our cousin"—you nodded politely at Lord Hamidas—"I believe my approach to be more… tactful. I know your methods, Brother. By taking Prophis by force after the Faction's coup, you would have made yourself an enemy of the city. And believe me, you don't want to be the enemy of Prophisians. My approach, instead, made me a heroine. In their view, I helped free the city. Now we can manipulate the entire Faction and the temple from within, without having to resort to violence. The people could support us, if I make them believe Lady Avasiannata's intentions were never to free the city, but to take it for herself."

He remained silent for a moment, thinking. At last he sighed and said, "I suppose your approach might work too," but his tone wasn't enthusiastic as you had hoped.

You swallowed apprehensively. You were walking a tightrope, trying to convince Elias of your good faith when all the facts pointed at your unequivocal betrayal.

"I understand your carefulness, and your hesitancy to trust me again," you said. "All I want is to be with you again and forget the past. I want to build a future with you. Tell me what I can do to prove my unconditional love and loyalty and I will do it." You bowed your head for a moment, longer than what etiquette required. "Anything."

He clasped his hands and gave you a defiant look. "You will give me my nuptial gift indeed," he said. "You will give me the city. To that end, you will kill Lady Avasiannata as proof of your love and loyalty. I will only agree to see you if you can bring her head to me."

You didn't answer. He knew about you and me. It was the

ultimate test. Of course, you wouldn't do it—if you had, how could I be talking to you now? Yet you had no choice but to agree to his request.

"I have never killed before," you said, almost adding *unlike you* but wisely keeping it to yourself, "and I don't believe this is a wise move considering how Prophisians came to trust Lady Avasiannata, but"—you raised your hand before he could argue—"I will do it if this is what it takes to prove my allegiance."

"Then we have an agreement," he said. "Come back here tomorrow, same time. Lord Hamidas will be expecting you. If indeed you bring what I am asking for, he will escort you across the sea to New Hyla, where I will meet you. Do not wear that sun-suit, or any other suit I offered you." He paused, waiting for you to nod in approval. He must have been worried you might use their powers against him, rightfully so after what happened in Prophis. So you nodded, which seemed to appease him. He nodded back and continued, "Should you fail—"

"I won't fail," you said firmly.

Elias gave you a smug smile. "I will see you tomorrow, then."

His hologram vanished, and Lord Hamidas picked up the holophone. You extended your hand toward him and said, with a flat voice, "Lord Hamidas."

"Your Highness," he answered as he shook your hand, sealing your agreement to meet again tomorrow.

You gave him a last look before turning away and leaving the warehouse. You would get the eggs back, and I would keep my head on my shoulders. How, you didn't know, but you had twenty-seven hours to figure it out.

THE HEAD WEIGHED heavy and pulled your shoulder muscles hard. It smelled terrible, too. A mix of decayed flesh and dried blood. The only thing that smelled worse was the *Rosebay*, the ship on which you had traveled from Arnitha to Phau. Thankfully, the bag covering the head concealed most of the smell, but your nose would never forget the horrid stench that made you gag as you placed the head inside it.

Your spirit felt tainted, too. Of course, you hadn't dealt the fatal blow to the person whose head lay inside the bag, and said person deserved to lose it, but it was still against your principles to cause someone's death. But reality has a unique way of forcing idealists to bend the rules they abide by. You didn't like it, yet you were ready to bend the rules so you could retrieve what Zephis had entrusted you with. Not only to obey your goddess, but to obey your conscience, too. You had a moral obligation to Celadon. You knew she would only find peace after her children had safely hatched in their native environment—and not in a serpentarium where they would become the slaves of both boredom and men.

Lord Hamidas gave you a surprised look when you entered the warehouse. "I must admit I didn't expect Your Highness to come today," he said.

If you hadn't felt so sullen, you would have snorted. "Yet here I am, delivering what was promised."

"Shall I take a look?" he asked, not sounding enthusiastic at the idea of seeing a decapitated head.

Nodding, you opened the bag. You winced and pinched your nose as the acrid and coppery smell of blood escaped and filled the room. Lord Hamidas winced too and quickly glanced inside the bag before stepping away and asking you to close it. "I can't believe you did it," he said. "You and

Lady Avasiannata were very close, I heard."

"Not as close as Elias and I are."

He cleared his throat. "I need to proceed to further examination before taking you to New Hyla," he said, taking a device out of his pocket. "I am sure you understand."

What he held in his hand was a gene-scanner, an advanced piece of technology able to establish someone's identity beyond any doubt. All rulers and their extended family had their blood drawn at birth or when they joined the family through marriage; their genes were cataloged and the information stored in an interstellar registry. The registry was used to prevent identity theft or to verify the claims of illegitimate children. Unsurprisingly, both my mother and I had been added to the registry shortly after joining the imperial family—whether we liked it or not— which meant you needed more than a Cleanser's illusion to pass off the head in the bag as mine.

Your mouth went dry as Lord Hamidas approached the bag with the device. "No need to open it again," he said, grimacing in disgust.

"Of course," you said. A gene-scanner didn't need to be in contact with the person—or what was left of them—to work. That's what made the device so impressive, but also what allowed you to trick it. You had used diaston from the governor's luxurious wardrobe to make the inside layer of the bag, a layer that you had soaked in a basin filled with my own blood.

You pursed your lips as you remembered how I bled the day before, so you could infuse the diaston with my blood. You hadn't forced me. I was actually the one who came up with this plan, but you still resented having to sacrifice someone else's life and see me suffer a major blood draw that weakened me so much I fainted during the procedure.

You knew it was the price of freedom—and I gladly paid it with my blood and the life of an imperial who wouldn't have hesitated to execute every single one of us for the glory of the empire—but you still felt uncomfortable scheming against your brother like he enjoyed scheming against his enemies. You wanted to be better than him, but you had no choice. You had to fight fire with fire.

Lord Hamidas activated the device and pointed it toward the bag. You held your breath in apprehension as the device's screen flashed an "*Error, please scan again*" message twice before it finally displayed my name and picture. Exhaling quietly, you followed Lord Hamidas outside of the warehouse to a small ship docked in Prophis's harbor.

You crossed the Auriverian Sea in silence, not exchanging a single word with the crew despite their insistent looks at you and the bag you carried. You were no more talkative during the ride from New Hyla's harbor to Larigny—the largest royal residence in Phau's Cician colony.

As the carriage went through Larigny's gates, you saw dozens of workers busying themselves inside the court-yard.

"What is all this commotion?" you asked Lord Hamidas.

"After your conversation with His Majesty, he ordered the construction of a new serpentarium here in Larigny."

Clenching your fists, you gave him a broad smile to hide the tension boiling inside your chest. Elias was already acting as if you were back. As if you and Celadon's children were *his*. If there was any trace left of fraternal love for your brother in your heart, it had just died.

You hated everything about the present moment and didn't know how you managed to hold yourself together. You had done your best to avoid the situation you found yourself in today, including helping revolutionaries take a foreign city you barely knew about not so long ago. And, you realized, that had led you exactly here. If you hadn't helped me and the Faction, if you hadn't shown us the suits, Numa would have never found you, and the eggs would still be safe inside your cache. Perhaps you would have brought them to their final nest in New Zankia. But, you also knew, we would have failed if you hadn't helped us. Your brother would have eliminated the Faction before moving to take Prophis, and eventually he would have found you or forced you to flee. It was as if no matter what you did, you were doomed to face Elias to settle your fate. If this wasn't destiny, you didn't know what was.

Larigny was a modest residence compared to Hyla's palace on Therria, but it was still worthy of a king. Walking inside its walls as you followed Lord Hamidas brought back memories of childhood vacations from what felt like a lifetime ago. But you couldn't let yourself be submerged in nostalgia. You had come here to get back what was yours and ensure Elias would never threaten you again.

Your right arm, where the miniaturizer was hidden under your sleeve, trembled nervously as Lord Hamidas opened the door leading to Elias's apartment, silently praying for the eggs to be here, in Larigny. What if Elias had left them on the *Lifebringer*? It would take more time for you to retrieve them. A few days, perhaps, of having to fake romantic feelings toward Elias until he would let you board a shuttle to the *Lifebringer*. In the meantime, I would have to keep hiding so people would genuinely believe I was dead, and who knew what move Elias would make on Prophis? What if Elias decided to marry you as soon as tomorrow? No, you had to retrieve the eggs and settle things with your brother today. Each passing hour in his company increased the risk of him discovering our ruse or making you his wife—or worse, both.

Elias was waiting for you in his reception room, nonchalantly lying on a velvet couch, as if your arrival wasn't that important.

"Isn't she beautiful?" he said to Lord Hamidas after sitting up and looking at you from head to toe. Per his request, you weren't wearing one of the suits he had gifted you. Instead, you wore a light blue dress embroidered with white pearls that I had given you. One of the last remnants of my past life.

You curtsied and said, "You look radiant too, Brother." You looked down as you pronounced those words, not daring to cross his gaze as you lied. You had fooled him in the past, but he had no reason to suspect you back then. Now he was on the lookout for any sign of betrayal.

He stood up and approached. "This," he said, pointing at the bag you had been carrying since Prophis, "is what I was promised, I suppose."

"The gene-scanner confirmed the identity, Your Majesty," Lord Hamidas said.

"Shall I see?"

You moved to open the bag, but Lord Hamidas said, "Is it really necessary, sir? The… smell is rather unpleasant."

Elias took a few steps back but still said, "I trust the device's reading, but I wish to see her. If only for an instant."

Holding your breath, you nodded and showed him the head. Thankfully, he didn't come closer. The illusion cast by Jovien was powerful, but worked best at a distance. Should Elias touch the head, it would fade and he would recognize the features of the governor.

"I have to admit you have good taste," Elias said as you put the head back in the bag. "She was a beautiful woman. I could have fallen for her, too."

You remained silent, not knowing how to answer.

"We should send it to the emperor, don't you think?" he added. "After I send our troops to take control of the city once you seize control of the Faction. As a peace offering, to show him we took down the traitor who claimed his city."

"Lady Avasiannata was the emperor's stepdaughter," Lord Hamidas pointed out.

"Don't you think I am aware, Lord Hamidas?" Elias said sharply, causing the emissary to lower his head. "If you knew the full extent of the relationship between the emperor and Lady Avasiannata, you would know that the emperor would send me a formal thank-you note for delivering him her head."

You doubted the emperor would receive the news as well as Elias imagined it, but you still said, "I think this is a brilliant idea, Elias. I shall send it myself. I am the one who killed her, after all."

He raised an eyebrow before saying, "But, of course, Cyrelle. It would be unfair of me to take credit for what you did. Tell me, how did you do it? Did you lure her to your bed before stabbing her to death? No, you strangled her during foreplay, right? Or did you poison her, maybe?"

The excitement that flashed in his eyes as he asked these questions made you want to vomit. Your brother was sicker than you had thought him to be. "I poisoned her," you said. Elias knew you too well to believe you would have killed someone using a violent method, no matter how aroused the idea made him.

"Poison, of course," he said, a smile on the corner of his lips. He turned to Lord Hamidas. "We are good, cousin. Please take my nuptial gift"—he gestured toward the bag—"and hand it over to a servant to store it in the freezer.

I wouldn't want the emperor to receive a rotten head."

You tensed as Lord Hamidas took the bag, but the disgusted wince on his face assured you he wouldn't open it to take a closer look. Then he left, leaving you and Elias alone.

"I heard you are building a new serpentarium," you said.

"I am indeed. I wouldn't be a good husband if I left my future wife at the mercy of a cruel goddess. Celadon's children will grow up on Phau, as Zephis wished, and they will serve us, as Eterion wished too. Everyone will be satisfied."

You brought your hands together in a prayer in front of your chest. "You are such a good man," you said. Then you asked, as innocently as you could, "May I see them?"

He nodded. "They are incubating in my bedroom."

You gulped. Elias's bedroom was the last place in the galaxy you wanted to go, but if the eggs were there, you had no choice. So you followed him, silently praying to Zephis, to Ystos, and to Eterion—why not, after all—for your ordeal to be soon over.

You entered Elias's bedroom and let out a quiet sigh of relief. The eggs were there indeed, resting inside an incubator. All you had to do was get them back and leave. It sounded so easy. But it wouldn't be enough, you knew. As long as Elias was alive, he would hunt you and Celadon's children.

"They will soon hatch," Elias said, looking at you. "You took good care of them. Perhaps Zephis was right in wanting them to be on Phau."

From his eyes shone a gleam of desire that turned your blood to ice. If he had restrained himself in the past, waiting for you to be married, that was now over.

Before he could make the first move, you took his hand and said, "I have another nuptial gift for you."

"I am already amply satisfied," he said, moving his head dangerously toward yours.

You evaded his kiss and pulled him toward the bed. "I can only imagine how difficult it has been for you. Organizing a wedding only to find your bride gone on the day she was meant to become your wife. Celadon's eggs and the future of the kingdom vanished. The agonizing pain you must have felt when you thought I had betrayed you. The long, desperate search across the galaxy, only to find me in someone else's arms. I know you hurt, Elias. And if I never intended to cause you such harm, I know I am responsible for it. That's why I must be the one chasing the pain away from your heart."

"It will be all gone when you become my wife," he said, sitting next to you on the bed.

You nodded. "I know, but I can make it go away sooner. I can offer you the most pleasurable experience in the galaxy, and I can offer it right now."

"Without a doubt," he said, putting his hand on your cheek.

You gave him a large smile. "Let me serene you, Brother. It is the least I can do after everything that happened."

He raised an eyebrow. It made you want to laugh and say *What did you expect?* but you kept smiling, waiting for him to pull himself together. Your skin was already touching his, so you could have established the spirit-bond right away, but getting his consent would allow you to delve deeper into his mind without fighting his efforts to repel you—for a time, at least.

"This isn't what I imagined, but it is a gift equally good that I can't refuse," he said at last.

Your heartbeat quickened. He had said yes, and it was now time to bring an end to your ordeal. This was your one and only chance. You couldn't give in, no matter how scared you were of the consequences.

As you looked at him, you remembered Marise, and your stomach clenched. You remembered the promise you had made to her, before serening her one last time. You wouldn't give serenity to those who didn't deserve it. Yet there you were, inside Elias's bedroom, ready to initiate a serening ritual with the least deserving person in the galaxy.

"Take my hands," you told him.

He did so, and as soon as his fingers clenched yours, you delved into his mind.

You looked for his deepest fears and his worst deeds and quickly brought them to the forefront of his mind. You could have taken your time to torment him, to make him pay for his actions, but you didn't. Nobody in Larigny heard him scream, for his cries for help echoed only in your mind.

You never told me what you saw, neither did you pen it down, and I never asked. What you found must have been terrible because you barely had to poison his mind with fictional images of his demise to cause his spirit to collapse. Amplifying what was already there with the power of your own mind was enough.

As his spirit crumpled, so did his body. You waited until his cries ceased and his entire spirit became silent before interrupting the spirit-bond. Opening your eyes, you found him petrified. His face was pale and his eyes hollow, as if life itself had been sucked out of them. You almost gasped, but restrained yourself. After taking a deep breath in, you moved his body into a supine position on the bed and stared at his empty gaze for a long moment. It was over.

You went to the incubator, collected the eggs, and carefully stored them in your miniaturizer one last time. The next time you restored them to their normal size, it would be in a nest in New Zankia.

Then, and only then, you screamed.

THE GUARDS FOUND you trembling on the floor. "The king fainted and won't wake up," you told them. "Go get a doctor, by all the gods!"

When physicians examined Elias, they found him unconscious and unresponsive, his heart beating so erratically it could stop at any moment. They rushed him to the closest clinic, where they resuscitated him once, but not twice. Only two hours after you had caused deep trauma to his body and spirit, they pronounced him dead.

You would have been the primary suspect if the autopsy had revealed anything suspicious, but there was nothing to explain the king's sudden death besides an odd stress-induced heart attack. And how could a frail, unarmed princess devoted to the Goddess of Serenity cause any harm? Nobody could seriously suspect you. Even your mother, who knew in her heart that you had caused her son's end, had a hard time believing you could have corrupted the serening ritual enough to kill someone.

Of course, you couldn't stay away from Cicia after what had happened. Not only was the king dead and did you have to attend his funerals, but you had become Cicia's queen, whether you liked it or not. The law was the law, and Elias having no children, you were the throne's heiress.

You had no desire to rule over the kingdom. I like to think it's because you had embraced my ideals and wished for Cician citizens to choose their own leaders, and it probably was, at least in part. But what you desired the most was to abdicate. What you couldn't stop dreaming about during your coronation was going back to Prophis to be with me every day and raising Celadon's children as your own on the planet where they belonged.

You almost did it. You almost abdicated, but believe it or not, I advised you not to. Not yet. If you abdicated now, your closest cousin would become the king, only to perpetuate the regime your ancestors had put in place. Nothing would change. Cicia needed its queen so it would eventually be freed of the monarchy. Until that day, because you didn't care about power, you were the best ruler Cician people could wish for. It is difficult for me to say these words, considering how I dislike monarchy itself, but I knew *you*, Cyrelle of Cicia, would make a *good queen*.

So you agreed to stay in power for the time being. Still eager to support my ideals, you thought about proclaiming the creation of a parliament, to which you would transfer most of your powers, but such an abrupt change so early after your coronation would have only brought you a regicide from one of your cousins eager to keep the crown's power intact. Half of them already secretly blamed you for Elias's death, though they couldn't explain how you did it. The disappearance of Lord Hamidas didn't help them trust you either. As he was the only person alive aware of my supposed death, you had no choice but to accuse him of treason and send him to the harshest Cician prison, where no one would ever listen to his tales. It made you feel bad at first to condemn a man to a fate worse than death, but when you signed the order, you reminded yourself that he had plotted with Elias to trick the Faction and cause my death. Yet it was a risky move, for your cousins held Lord Hamidas in high esteem. They didn't dare challenge your order only because they feared for their own lives; but you couldn't count on fear to keep them at bay forever. Should you push them to the edge with too many threats or bold decisions, they wouldn't hesitate to move against you with deadly means. Both your position and your life were fragile, and I had no desire to see a picture of your bloodied body lying next to Cicia's throne in the news.

Keeping you on the throne also ensured Prophis would remain a free city, a place where we could build a future together once the burden of leadership and divine duties left us. Shortly after Elias's death, the emperor moved to retake the city, but you sent Cician troops to protect us, recognizing our independence, and the Faction as Prophis's rightful transition leaders. To appease the emperor, you agreed to sell him diastium at cost for five Therrian years. A high price that you were willing to pay if it ensured my dream would prosper and my life would be spared.

While you took control of the kingdom's affairs, you didn't renege on your promise to your goddess. Searching your father's notes, you found the place where Celadon had been captured, which was close to the area you had already identified while studying maps in Prophis. It wasn't far from the city, which meant you had to ensure Prophis remained free from the empire so Celadon's children wouldn't be captured by the emperor, who was as greedy as your late brother. All Cician eyes were also on you, watching your every move, your every decision. You couldn't easily leave the palace while counselors kept chasing you day and night. You needed time—time to settle down in your new responsibilities, time for the political turmoil to wane—but Zephis didn't see it that way. She is a demanding goddess, and her patience was exhausted. She didn't care that being a new queen prevented you from acting faster. Quite the opposite. She was furious.

What nobody knew, not even me until recently, was that your own spirit had been deeply affected by what you did to Elias. The instant you had interrupted the spirit-bond, you had felt it. A curse. Cast upon you by none other than Zephis herself. She hadn't needed to send you a vision for it to be clear. It filled your spirit like a disease filling your body. Because you were still in Larigny, standing next to your dying brother, you kept a cool head and ignored the goddess's fury. You would deal with it later. Surely, you could pray to Zephis to explain why you had committed such an atrocity. It was only to follow her orders. Unless, perhaps, the goddess didn't think the ends justified the means as your mother had believed, or she had already been disappointed in you too many times. After everything you had done—lying about a vision, causing Celadon's death in her name, letting the eggs get stolen by Numa— corrupting the ritual to murder someone and becoming queen yourself was the last straw. Maybe she would never forgive you.

The curse was like a slow, painful death. Not the death of your body, not the death of your spirit, but the death of your very self. Each passing day, you woke up with fewer memories, and only your diary helped you remember your past, your royal duties, and your recent decisions so your entourage wouldn't see your decline—myself included, for I didn't realize your state until it was too late.

Some days, you wore your powerful suits, hoping the contact of diaston against your skin would remind you of everything you had been through. It didn't work, but at least it helped conceal the truth a bit longer. Under the radiance of the sun-suit, your counselors still saw you as the queen they served, and not as a cursed woman who couldn't lead her country anymore.

Eventually you feared you couldn't use your suits anymore. What if you misused their powers, forgetting what the controllers did? You could torch the entire palace with the sun-suit or crush yourself to death with the moon-suit. So one day, you took the three suits Elias had gifted you to the Temple of Serenity and asked your mother to watch over them. When she asked why, you pretended you didn't want to keep anything that reminded you of your late brother, and mostly importantly, you explained that you didn't need them anymore. You didn't need to be as charismatic as Elias or as influential as he was. You weren't a queen consort living in the shadow of a king. You were the queen, the one and only ruler of Cicia—at least as long as the monarchy continued. You were enough.

What you didn't give your mother was the snake-suit. She didn't ask you why you kept it. She is your mother, after all, and knows you well. You had lived as Green Scales for too long to part with the suit. It also reminded you of your promise to bring Celadon's children to New Zankia, which you still planned to keep, as soon as your royal duties allowed it. But Zephis didn't intend to let you do it on your own terms. She had other, darker plans for you.

Unsurprisingly, the only piece of your memories that remained strongly anchored into your brain and grew more vivid as the time passed was that promise to bring the eggs back to Phau. Zephis, in her impatience and anger, was slowly but surely effacing every part of you that wasn't solely dedicated to keeping the promise you had made.

One morning, you woke up not remembering a single thing about yourself. All you knew was that you were Green Scales, the guardian of two soon-to-hatch snakes. Your diary-screen was there, lying on the nightstand next to you. You read it and realized the situation had gone too far. You couldn't continue pretending you were all right. You had to slip away from Hyla and go back to Phau, and then to the savanna, where you would finally find peace. The kingdom, your responsibilities, your plans for a future Cician democracy and for Prophis's prosperity, all that had become secondary.

You put your snake-suit on and, once more, took the eggs and disappeared from the palace.

My surprise was immense when I saw you on my doorstep, your snake-mask on. I hadn't expected to see you that day, wearing a suit I thought you didn't need anymore, but was thankful for the impromptu visit. We didn't see each other enough to my liking, for we were both busy with our new responsibilities, so I didn't complain. I eagerly welcomed you with a long embrace. I hoped we would spend the night talking about our plans for the future—a future where I hoped to wake up next to you every morning. But we didn't talk about our plans, or the future, or anything at all.

A part of you remembered the love you had for me and had felt compelled to see me before your last journey. I had never seen you so disoriented, my love. You were holding the diary firmly against your chest, as if it was the most precious thing in the world. You spent the night with me, barely speaking, answering my questions with desperate looks and passionate kisses. The next morning, you were gone. I thought you had left for the Cician colony, to Larigny probably, but then I found your diary. You had left it behind, right by my side on the bed, unlocked, an invitation to open it. When I read it, tears rolled down my cheeks. I searched for you in the city, but you were nowhere to be found. You were already on your way to

New Zankia. I desired only to follow you, but I had to find a cure first, if I wanted to help you.

At first, I didn't know how to. How does a mere human break a curse cast by an angry goddess? I could have prayed to Zephis myself, but she would have ignored me. I wasn't one of her followers. I wasn't pious enough to deserve any god's attention. But I knew people who were, and who also had the favor of another god—one who was known for his dislike of corruption and his sense of justice, one who didn't hesitate to confront his equals when they were guilty of the sins he cleansed humans from. One you had served, even if only briefly.

I went to the Temple of Purity and told everything to the High Priestess and to Jovien. Together, we prayed to Ystos, who eventually agreed to help us lift the curse because you had helped cleanse the corruption in the city, and because Zephis's punishment was overtly cruel, corrupting your soul despite everything you had done to please her. It was risky for the god to move against another goddess, but it wasn't his first time, and these divine quarrels didn't concern us. All we cared about was that we had a cure. Except, for the cure to work, you first had to remember. Not your entire life, of course, but enough of yourself and of the events that had led Zephis to cast the curse on you.

We scoured New Zankia for weeks. Thankfully, you had left behind your notes and maps, narrowing our search area, but it still felt like looking for a needle in a haystack.

I didn't know how you could survive there. The savanna is so large, its climate so brutal. But Zephis is a cunning goddess. She wanted the curse to last, so she provided you with everything you needed. Vark was the first to spot you, and as soon as we knew where your den was, I went in at night. You were sleeping in your snake-suit, two small snakes cuddled against you, enjoying your warmth and feeling their mother's scales. A stream of fresh water flowed inside your den so you wouldn't go thirsty, and food appeared out of a horn you had no memory of finding.

I sat in the entrance until the morning, not daring to approach you. The snakes were only babies, but I still feared their reaction if I tried waking you up. Also, I feared *your* reaction. Would you remember me? Would you attack me, thinking I was an intruder here to abduct Celadon's children?

To my relief, you didn't attack me when you saw me. You gestured to the snakes to stay quiet and invited me inside. "I don't know who you are, stranger," you said, your voice hoarse, not used to pronouncing words anymore, "but I know within me that you are a friend."

My heart ached, but I smiled. Yes, I was a friend, and so much more than that.

You know what happens next. I've been with you for five days now, sharing your meals and getting to know Reseda and Viridiane, Celadon's daughters. I've told you everything I know, and the gentle smile on your face tells me you believe me. You remember, don't you?

Cicia needs its queen. Your counselors have done their best to manage the kingdom's affairs in your absence, but your cousins are already scheming to usurp your throne and ruin our dream. Our dream, for I hope we will, once all this is over, finally build a home together on the hills where we will watch the sun rise over the Auriverian Sea.

I need you to drink this. It will cleanse the curse from your spirit. It won't hurt, I promise. I'm not asking you to abandon Reseda and Viridiane. They can fend for themselves, but I know they love you and you love them. You went through the stars for them. You will be free to visit them whenever you want as queen of Cicia.

I don't know if Zephis will seek more revenge, but we aren't alone against her wrath. Your mother has been praying for you. After losing you not once, but twice, all your mother wants is your happiness. You can finally live and love who your heart desires.

Zephis has taken enough from you. Everyone has taken enough from you.

Hold my hand while you drink, my love. Drink, and be yourself again.

AUTHOR'S NOTE

WHAT IS THE color of time?

I found myself wondering this when I was seventeen years old, reading "Peau d'Âne" by Charles Perrault for the first time, in high school literature. In the original French tale, the protagonist tries to dodge an incestuous union with her father by asking for dresses of the color of the sun, the moon, and… *du temps*. In French, *temps* has two meanings: *weather* and *time*. I was, like most of my classmates, utterly confused. A dress of the color of the weather? But the weather fluctuates. It can be blue when it's sunny, gray when it's cloudy, white when it snows… And as for time? Time doesn't have a color, does it?

Our teacher quickly explained that Perrault meant *weather* as in "a clear blue sky" hence why in the English translation the protagonist asks for a dress of the color of the sky. Though it clarified the story's meaning, the idea of the color of time stuck with me. As soon as I decided to write this retelling, I knew its title before anything else.

The other element from the original tale that stuck with me was its profoundly unfair ending. If you are familiar with the tale, you may wonder what I mean by "unfair." After all, the protagonist avoids marrying her father and, after many twists and turns, marries the prince of the foreign country in which she had found refuge. Her hardship is over, virtue prevailed, and the moral of the story is that no matter how difficult it is, you should always do the right thing—in Donkeyskin's case, not marrying her father even if it means living as a poor kitchen girl hiding under a donkey skin. But what about the king, her father? Not only had he wanted to force her daughter to marry him, but he forced her to flee and live a miserable life to escape her terrible fate. Shouldn't he be punished for what he did? At the very least, apologize and beg for forgiveness? No. In the original tale, he appears at his daughter's wedding as if nothing happened, nobody holds him accountable, and he doesn't apologize. Everything is forgotten.

It made me furious. Not at Perrault, because his choice made sense. Rulers, in particular monarchs, rarely apologize for their behavior nor are they held accountable for their crimes. But I was furious nonetheless, and I knew that my Donkeyskin would get justice for what happened to her—and ideally, she would get justice for herself, and not thanks to a prince rescuing her. Let's also not forget this poor donkey who gets slaughtered for nothing.

Many years after I read the original tale, I came across a call for short story submissions. The theme: fairy-tales in space. Immediately, I thought of Perrault's "Donkeyskin" and the concept of the suits unfolded in my mind. I was excited and decided to make it a novel and not a short story. I already had a title and a goal (getting justice for the protagonist and the sacrificed magical animal). What else did I need? Something bigger. I didn't want this story to be solely about Cyrelle. I had recently seen Denis Villeneuve's *Dune* and loved the blend of science fiction and fantasy, the character of Lady Jessica, and the overarching theme of the saga. It became, after the original tale, my biggest inspiration for *The Color of Time*. Cyrelle's mother is a combination of the fairy godmother and Lady Jessica. Celadon and diastium are reminiscent of sandworms and spice. Phau and its people suffering under the rule of unjust rulers should remind you of Arrakis. But there is no Paul, for I wanted this story to be about collective action. Frank Herbert's message was this: beware of heroes. I listened. There is no hero in *The Color of Time*, only people working together for a better future.

The color of time needed to be more than a punny title, of course. You should now know that the color of time is green like diastium or Celadon's skin. I didn't pick this color for a particular reason besides it sounded right to me for a giant snake from space. It is only later that I realized green is the color of US dollar bills, and if time is money, as many people say, then it is an apt choice.

So now time has in color in my mind. I hope it also does have one in yours, and that it is a beautiful viridian green.

ACKNOWLEDGMENTS

AS ALWAYS, I open my acknowledgments by thanking my spouse Félix. This is particularly needed for this book because I could not have finished it without him. My father passed away while I was in the middle of the first draft, and the chaos that ensued—jumping on a plane, dealing with everything, and my anxiety going through the roof leading to a bad bout of depression—made it seem impossible to finish. Thankfully, with his help, things got better and I completed the first draft of what eventually became the book you are holding in your hands.

Next I want to thank Claire Rudy Foster, who was the first person to believe in this manuscript and in my writing in general. Thank you. Then comes my publishers, Brianne Shiraki and Josh Sutphin. Brianne's developmental and line edits, as well as her vision for this book, were phenomenal. It wouldn't be what it is today without all her hard work. As for Josh, this wouldn't be such a beautiful book without his artistic vision and well-designed creative brief. While I'm talking about art, a huge thank to Alyssa Winans who created the cover art. It had always been a dream to get Alyssa to do a cover for one of my books, and wow, I can't believe it actually happened?! It's so good! Thank you so much. The interior design is also fabulous, thanks to Morgan Wodring who brought Celadon to life in the chapter headers and designed the cute little snake dingbat. Thank you, friend. Also, big thanks to Kaitlin Schmidt for the incredible copyedits.

None of this would have been possible without my agent, A.J. Van Belle, who deserves all the kudos in the world for being such a great champion of my work—and a great person, period. Thank you for believing in this unusual story and bringing it to the wonderful folks at Shiraki Press. I am so fortunate to have you by my side in my writing career.

Obligatory thanks to all my friends who support my writing and my unhingedness: Florence Chien, Morgan Wodring, L.N. Holmes, Linda Stewart; the Book Inkers folks, always; Andrea, Christina, Katie, Ryan, Essa, Camille, Holly, Kemi, and Julie for helping me choose between cover compositions when I was agonizing over it (because Alyssa is so good, how can you choose just one?); in addition to the previous list, Tina, Victoria, Nikhil, Julia, and all my fellow Cheese Rangers; the #SmallPitch folks for making me laugh and cry and for being the best online community I've ever encountered; my agent siblings for always being here to support my releases (I can't wait to read YOUR books!).

Last but not least, to you, for reading this book. You are the reason I keep writing. Thank you.

Photo by Clayton J. Mitchell

MILLIE ABECASSIS IS a French author of fantasy, fairy-tale retellings, science fiction, and horror. She is a graduate of the Panthéon-Sorbonne University and now works in the biotech industry. She resides in San Jose, California with her spouse, their cats, and too many plants to care for. When she isn't reading or writing, you can find her playing video games or in her backyard trying to stop her wisterias from taking over the world. You can learn more about her writing and other endeavors at www.millieabecassis.com.

CONTRIBUTORS

Written by Millie Abecassis
MILLIEABECASSIS.COM

Author representation by A.J. Van Belle
The Booker Albert Literary Agency
THEBOOKERALBERTAGENCY.COM

Edited by Brianne Shiraki
SHIRAKIPRESS.COM

Copyedited by Kaitlin Schmidt
KAITLIN-SCHMIDT.COM

Cover illustration by Alyssa Winans
ALYSSAWINANS.COM

Interior illustration by Morgan Wodring

Book design by Josh Sutphin
SHIRAKIPRESS.COM

This book was created entirely by humans.
No generative AI was used for any part of its production.